The Anthology of Cozy-Noir

**Edited by
Andrew MacRae**

DARKHOUSE
BOOKS

The Anthology of Cozy-Noir
All rights reserved

These stories are works of fiction. Any resemblance between events, places, or characters, within them, and actual events, organizations, or people, is but happenstance.

No part of this book may be reproduced or transmitted in any form or by any means, electronic or mechanical, including photocopying, recording, or by any information storage and retrieval system, without permission in writing from the publisher.

Copyright © 2014 by Darkhouse Books

ISBN 978-0-9908428-0-4

First published November 17, 2014
Published in the United States of America

Darkhouse Books
160 J Street, #2223
Niles, California 94539

Table of Contents

Introduction

Welcome to "The Anthology of Cozy-Noir" – Darkhouse Book's fledgling attempt in publication. The world of publishing is changing at a speed never before experienced in a major industry. What were unchallengeable rules a scant five years ago are now relicts of an earlier age. How-To books for self-publishing are out of date three months after they are released. Monster-sized companies fight over who will be in control while their skirmishes imperil readers and writers alike.

At the same time, it has never been easier to publish a book, and each of the millions being published every year testifies to that ease. And it is into this world of flux and turmoil that we release our first volume of prose, "The Anthology of Cozy-Noir".

It is a perilous project to introduce a new sub genre, doubly so when the name selected is at surface, and a deep surface at that, self-contradicting. Confusion and concern among a segment of our community yet for many of us there is an 'ah ha' moment on first hearing the term. "Yes," they cry, "That's exactly what it is."

At least there is no confusion from the name itself, for "Cozy-Noir" aptly captures that odd and difficult to make out the juncture of two disparate styles of writing. And, at essence, that is really what Cozy-Noir is all about.

In this anthology we present thirteen stories that in some way or shape, illuminate through quality word craft, a shadow or two in this murky meeting place.

Cozy-Noir embraces noir's mood indigo, rain-slick streets, where underworlds and overlords do commerce and the PI plays the part of the reluctant knight errant. Happy endings are banished to the basement, while existential angst makes itself at home with a bottle of beer at the kitchen table.

At the same time, Cozy-Noir blends in strong tasting elements from the kitchen where cozies are created. A well-defined sense of community, an interesting cast of characters, interesting location, while keeping the nastier bits of detective fiction, such as corpses of murder victims and the violence done, off page and out of sight.

We hope you enjoy these stories.

Andrew MacRae
September, 2014
Niles, California

We begin this anthology with a story from Robert Lopresti, a prolific writer with more than fifty published stories, including Black Orchid Novella and Derringer Award winners. His novel, "Such a Killing Crime" is published by Kearney Street Books.

In this story, Mr. Lopresti introduces us to the owners and patrons of a small pizza café in mainstream, main street, Middle America. It is a place where, for some people, life is about to take an interesting turn.

The Roseville Way

by Robert Lopresti

The first time the tall man came in, Mary had plenty of time to look him over. It was mid-afternoon on a Tuesday and he was the only customer in the place.

He was thin but muscular, with slick black hair, and the kind of skin they call olive-colored. He ordered two slices with extra cheese and sat down in the back to eat them.

A minute later he was on his feet, eyes wide. The way he shot back to the counter Mary was afraid there was something wrong with the food.

He leaned across the counter to Cliff, who was working the dough. "Where you from?"

Cliff looked up but didn't take his attention off his work. "What do you mean? I live here."

"Uh uh. Which borough? You didn't learn to make pizza like this west of the Hudson."

Cliff grinned and Mary relaxed. "Hey, doll," he said. "We got a connoisseur."

"A man of taste," she agreed.

"You spotted me, Chief. My uncle ran a pizzeria back east in Brooklyn. I did my apprenticeship there and we moved out here last fall to try our own place."

"Well, you know your stuff." The tall man paused to crease his slice down the middle and take a bite. "I never expected to get anything like this out here in the sticks."

"Careful," said Cliff. "My wife—the lady scowling at you—was born and raised here."

The stranger nodded at Mary. "No offense. I'm trying to compliment you guys."

She couldn't help but smile. "Are you just passing through?"

"Nah. Gonna be here a while." His narrow face brightened. "Maybe longer than I expected, considering how good the fare is."

After he left Mary said what a nice surprise it had been.

"Yeah," said Cliff, shifting on his stool to take the weight off his bad leg. "But maybe it just shows our problem."

"What do you mean?"

"Maybe we're a thousand miles from our audience. Everybody in the Midwest is happy to eat MegaPizza." That was what they called the two chains that had built big joints on the highway just after Cliff's New York Style had opened on Main Street.

Mary looked at the man she had loved ever since they met when she went east to try art school. Art hadn't worked out but the marriage had survived that, and the accident, and she hoped it would glide through a little business slump.

<hr>

The tall man returned that evening and ordered an extra large pizza with sausage. "I'll be back in half an hour. Can you save the last booth for me?"

"Sure," said Mary. The place was only half full and few people wanted to sit at the far end of the narrow storefront anyway.

He returned just as Cliff slipped the peel, the long wooden paddle, into the oven to remove the pie. With him was an older man, built like a wrestler, Mary thought. He was short, muscular, with a full head of graying hair and a nose that had been broken.

He looked around the pizzeria with bright eyes that seemed to pay more attention than most newcomers. Then, with a nod to his companion, he walked over to Mary. "How you doing, miss? You sell wine here?"

"Wine and beer."

"Great. We'll have a bottle of your best red."

Mary told him the price, because it was more than most people in Roseville would expect to pay with a pizza. The gray-haired man didn't blink. "Fine. Just bring it back to us." And he strolled to the last booth as if he had been there a hundred times.

The tall man paid and, with Mary, brought everything to the booth.

She took care of a couple of other customers and then the older man was back, a big grin on his face. "Nick was right about you guys. This is freaking good pizza."

Except he didn't say freaking.

Mary frowned at him. "I'll thank you not to use that kind of language in here."

The tall man—Nick—stared at her in amazement. The older guy looked baffled, as if he couldn't figure out what had offended her.

"Now, you listen--" said Nick, and his tone made Cliff move closer.

The older man silenced him with a wave. "She's right, Nick. When in Roseville, do as the, Rosevillians?"

"Rosevillites," she said promptly.

"Exactly. I'm sorry, miss. I'll watch my tongue." He smiled. "We want to stay on your good side."

"I'm glad you like the food, Mister—"

"Vince. Just call me Vince."

Vince and his tall companion sat in the back booth for another two hours, chatting, laughing occasionally, and finishing the wine. When they got up Mary found money on the table.

"You left these," she called.

Vince waved a hand. "We took up your booth all night. Consider it a tip."

"How much, doll?" Cliff asked once the door had closed.

"More than their bill."

"Wow. Let's hope they come back."

They did. Not every night, but three or four times a week. Nick never again spoke as much as he had in the excitement of discovering Cliff's pizza. His boss, on the other hand, was always chatty. Vince explained that he was a businessman from the east coast, retired for health reasons.

"He's a mobster," Cliff said at home one night.

"You don't know that," said Mary. "And even if he was, he isn't now, is he? He's just a nice old man who's good for business."

And that was certainly true. Customers started coming more often. Maybe it was just that people were reluctant to enter if the place was empty. Maybe the two Italian-looking men in the back seemed to be a guarantee of quality, like truckers at a diner.

Whatever it was, they could now pay most of the bills without juggling credit cards.

About a month later Nick arrived early to place the order. "Three extra large, Mary. Mix up the toppings. And two kinds of wine."

"Special occasion?"

"Guests."

They came with Vince, three men in their thirties, all wearing suits better than you could buy in Roseville. Mary watched them talking in the back and thought how pleased and animated Vince looked.

At the end of the evening the guests left in a flurry of handshakes and Vince came over to settle the bill.

"You're probably wondering who the city slickers were."

"Any friends of yours are welcome, Vince."

"Thanks, Mary." His eyes were twinkling. "I love Roseville hospitality. You see, my nephew Jess took over the business when I retired. He sends people out sometimes to see how I'm doing."

"That's sweet," said Mary.

"That's not the only reason," said Nick. "Jess is smart enough to know where to go for advice when he has a tough problem."

Vince looked pleased. "He's a good kid."

———————————

Two days later Donny Carpenter came in. His long form was slumped and swaying slightly. Drunk again. Mary sucked in her breath.

Donny had been trouble ever since he left the army. The first time he had been in the pizzeria he had noticed Cliff's limp and asked: "Got that in the war?"

"My leg? No."

"Then what happened?"

Mary saw Cliff's face; and knew how much he hated to talk about it. She tried to interrupt but Donny waved her off.

"Let him talk. What happened, pizza man?"

"I fell down some steps."

"Yeah? I had some buddies in Fallujah who fell down a flight of stairs. People were shooting at them. Anyone ever shoot at you, pizza man?"

Mary thought Cliff was going to tell him that the mugger who knocked him down a flight of subway steps had a knife not a gun. But Cliff just stared at him.

By the time the drunk left her husband was in a bad mood that didn't lift for a week. Donny didn't come back often, but when he did it meant trouble.

But this night Vince happened to be in and Nick was on his feet almost before the door closed. If Mary had any doubt that he was a bodyguard, it vanished at that moment.

"What's today's special, Mary Mary?" said Donny, smirking. He stood at the counter, sliding one hand slowly over the top of the cash register.

She could feel Cliff stiffening beside her. She smiled, trying to ease the moment. "Extra large with all the toppings for the price of a regular, Donny."

"All those I-tie things," he said. "Anchovies! What kind of food is that?"

"You're drunk," said Cliff. "Get out."

"You gonna make me, Cliffie? You and what army?" He laughed. "I forgot. You never served in the army. Nobody around here was dumb enough for that, except me. Nobody …"

"He asked you to leave," said Vince. He was on his feet and had pushed Nick aside.

Donny scowled. "Stay out of this, old man."

Vince grinned as he stepped forward. "I'm in it, sonny."

"Everybody calm down," said Cliff, but he didn't sound calm.

Donny was four inches taller, and at least thirty years younger. When Vince was a foot away Donny leaned back and unleashed a huge swing with his right fist.

Vince shifted his head and the blow barely brushed his face. He rocked on his heels but didn't back up. Mary thought he could have dodged the punch completely if he had chosen.

His smile widened. "The first one's free, son. The next one you pay for."

Donny swore and swung again. This time Vince ducked it easily and, coming in under the arm, hit the younger man below the ribs.

Donny folded over, air whooshing out, eyes filled with tears.

Vince advanced, hands wrapped together to form a club. He raised them above his head. Mary gasped.

"Boss, no," said Nick. His tone was quiet, conversational.

Vince straightened up, blinking like a man waking from a dream.

A dream he enjoyed, Mary thought.

He put a hand on Donny's shoulder. "You okay, son?" He acted as if the younger man had slipped and bumped his head.

Together Nick and Vince steered him to the last booth. Mary brought over a glass of water.

"Thanks," said Vince. "Clear this stuff away, okay?" He nodded to the wine bottle and glasses. Mary removed them without a word.

"Should we call the cops?" she whispered to Cliff, who was watching with fascination.

"Nah."

"But Donny's going to be mad."

"Just watch."

They did. Donny stared at Vince when he recovered. "How did you slip that punch?"

The older man shrugged. "It's an old trick. I'll show you sometime when you're sober. You were in the army?"

"Yeah. You?"

"I never had the privilege. Where did you serve?"

And they talked until closing time.

A week later someone asked the question that was on everybody's mind. Vince was sitting in his usual place, reading the paper. His old fashioned reading glasses slid down his nose, making him look older. Maybe that was what gave the kids the nerve.

Half a dozen high school students had come in for an after-school slice and sat near the front of the store, staring at Vince and giggling. Finally the ringleader, Bo Johnson, got double-dared into walking to the back of the shop.

"Hey, Vince."

"Hey, son. How's it shaking?"

"It's okay." Bo looked back at his friends who watched and laughed. "Can I ask you a question?"

"It's a free country."

Bo licked his lips. "Are you a godfather?"

The older man looked surprised. "As a matter of fact, I am."

"Really?"

"Yup. I have a godson almost your age and a cute little goddaughter." He patted his sports coat. "I think I've got pictures."

"No," said Bo. He glanced at his companions for support. "I mean, are you in the Mafia?"

"Hey," said Nick, "stop bothering the man."

"It's okay," said Vince. He pushed his glasses back up his face. "You kids watch too much TV. You think all Italian-Americans are mobsters?"

"Are you?" called one of the girls.

Vince's shoulders rose and for a moment Mary thought he was going to lose his temper.

Then he seemed to relax. "I'm just a retired businessman."

"What kind of business?" asked Bo.

Vince looked thoughtful. He tapped his newspaper with one big finger. "You kids read the news much?"

Solemnly, they shook their heads.

"You ought to. Pretty soon you'll be running the world and if you don't pay attention you'll do as bad a job as us old fools have done. There's a story on the front page today about a respectable businessman whose company went bankrupt and took about a thousand people's pensions down the tubes. The lawyers are arguing about whether he has to go to jail before his appeals are finished. Meanwhile, he's still living in a house that cost five million bucks."

Vince stood up, giving him a better view of the kids. "Then there's a story about a congressional hearing they're holding tomorrow, where another respectable businessman is gonna try to explain why his company overcharged the Pentagon by, I don't know, half a billion."

He let that sink in. Then he shrugged. "So to answer your question: I wasn't that kind of businessman. Hey Cliff, how about a pepperoni pizza for my friends here?"

"I'm a vegetarian," said the Logan girl.

"Good for you, sunshine. You'll live longer. Half and half, Cliff."

But the most surprising convert, Mary thought, was Mrs. Swoboda, who seemed to dislike everybody. She was short enough to have to look up at Vince, a seventyish gray-haired force of nature with a bag full of knitting in one hand, a cup of coffee in the other, and a harsh word for everybody.

Vince had been bragging about his nephew Jess, who had sent him a set of Fred Astaire movies on DVD. Vince loved Fred Astaire.

"It's nice your family cares about you," said Mrs. Swoboda. She came in twice a week for a meatball hoagie, and grumbled about the price every time. "My no-good children never call, much less send a present."

"Would that be the people I saw you with in the park a couple of weeks ago?" Vince asked. "The nice looking couple with the beautiful daughter?"

Mrs. Swoboda stood a little straighter. "Yes. That's my son and his family."

"So they do visit."

She shook her gray head. "Hardly ever. And they're the best of the brood, believe me. My daughter's kids are monsters. Her son Lionel—and what kind of a name is that to give a child?—is a nasty little fibber. If Lying Lionel tells you the sun is shining, you better bring an umbrella."

"Well, that just makes it more important that you're part of their lives," said Vince. "To show them what's right."

Behind Mrs. Swoboda's back Nick sighed and rolled his eyes.

"Ha! They don't listen to me. They all think I'm too boring to live."

When the older woman had toddled off Vince came up to the counter, shaking his head and smiling.

"Was she bothering you?" Mary asked.

"Bothering? Not a bit. She's a sweetheart."

"A sweetheart?" repeated Cliff. "She drives everyone crazy."

"Well, I like her." He laughed. "I like everybody in Roseville. I'm nuts about this town."

"What's the attraction?" asked Mary. "Beside the pizza, I mean."

"How can I put this?" Vince stared off for a moment. "Life is slow here. I don't mean boring. It's relaxed. People have time to talk to each other. To care about each other."

"That's the Roseville way," said Mary.

Nick snorted.

"You aren't buying it," said Cliff.

"People here are too nice." He waved a hand. "No offense, boss. I'm glad this place is good for you, but if it gets any slower I'll sleep on my feet."

Vince grinned. "Nick's job is to keep people safe. He's real good at it, but he doesn't feel needed here."

"Well, watch out at the corner of Main and Garden," said Cliff. "Some of those high school kids drive like lunatics."

The tall man sighed.

<hr>

Back home that night Mary asked: "Do you agree with Nick?"

Cliff was bent over, taking the brace off his leg. "About what, doll?"

"That Roseville is too slow."

He thought about it. "I used to think that when I first came to visit, after we got engaged. But this thing—" He tapped his leg. "I guess it slowed me down to your speed. Besides, I guess the city turned out to be too dangerous for me, didn't it?"

"You got mugged. It could have happened to anybody."

He turned away, hanging up his belt. "Does it bother you that I can't stand up for myself? Couldn't fight with Donny, or some other fool?"

"Fool is the right word for people who try to settle arguments with their fists." Standing behind Cliff, she put her arms around him. "I can be dangerous too, you know."

He kissed her hands. "Prove it."

It was on a Monday a few weeks later that two men from the east coast arrived just after the dinner rush—which on Monday, hardly existed anyway.

"Aw hell," said Donny. He was sitting in a booth, nursing a root beer.

"You can't have him to yourself every night," Mary reminded him.

"Yeah, I know. But when his nephew sends people it's like we don't exist."

"You really enjoy his company, don't you?"

"Yeah. He helps me stay, you know …"

She nodded. Donny had fallen off the wagon only once since Vince arrived. He had seen the young man stagger into the pizza shop one day and listened to no excuses. "Come back when you're feeling better," was all he had said, and turned away. Shamefaced, Donny had left, and returned two days later, sober.

Now he sat glaring at the two men in New York suits.

"Where does Vince usually sit?" asked the taller man. He had carrot red hair and a big smile.

"Booth in the back," said Cliff. "Want something while you wait?"

Red looked at his companion, a shorter man with a buzz cut and a damaged ear. "Hey, why not? A large pepperoni and two beers."

Cliff had just popped their pie into the oven when Mrs. Swoboda arrived to order a meatball hoagie and complain about her daughter-in-law, who had been terribly rude on the phone.

The two newcomers didn't settle into the booth. They stood near the back wall, examining a mural of the Coliseum, one of the few results of Mary's year in art school.

The door opened and Nick walked in. "Hey, Mary, if anybody comes--" He froze, eyes wide, looking at the two men in the back. All three men reached swiftly into their jackets.

Guns, thought Mary. They're going to shoot it out right here.

Then she saw Mrs. Swoboda, still standing at the counter, frowning and oblivious, a perfect human shield for Nick. She saw him realize the same thing.

For half a heartbeat Nick's face held an agony of indecision. Then he took two big steps to the side, taking the old woman out of the equation.

He fired the first shot just as Cliff crashed on top of Mary, landing them both on the floor behind the counter.

By the time she got her breath back the shooting had stopped and Mrs. Swoboda was screaming her head off.

"Everybody on their feet," yelled the redhead, moving swiftly. Mary heard a noise that she later realized was a gun being kicked. "And you, grandma, stop yelling. You aren't hurt."

"You okay?" whispered Cliff. Mary nodded.

The short one was looking over the counter. "You heard the man. Get up."

Mary helped Cliff to his feet. He tried to push her away but it was clear that the tumble had done his leg no good.

"What the hell are you doing?" asked Red.

Donny had pulled out his cell phone. "Put it on the table," said Shorty. When he did, Shorty smashed it with the butt of his gun.

Red looked at Cliff and Mary. "Get into the booths, you two. No, each in a separate one. Can't you move any faster?"

"His leg hurts," Mary blurted. The look Cliff gave her made her wish she had stayed quiet.

"You got a boo-boo?" asked Shorty. "Get over there or you'll find out what pain is."

Cliff limped to the booth next to Mary. Mrs. Swoboda had stumbled into another and Donny at the end completed the set.

Mary was amazed that none of the bullets had shattered the front window, but she realized that that was because Nick had moved to the side, away from Mrs. Swoboda. The bullets that missed him had hit the wall, not the glass.

And now she had no choice to look at the man they had all stepped over to get from the counter to the booths.

Nick lay on his back, eyes closed, not moving. There were at least two bullet holes in his chest but most of the blood seemed to be coming from under him.

Red moved Nick's gun to his own belt. "Okay," he said. "Everybody just calm down. Nobody's gonna make any calls, and nobody's going anywhere. You, soldier boy."

Donny was wearing his fatigue jacket. "Drag Nick into the back room there."

"Go to hell," said Donny.

Shorty stepped forward, grinning. He raised his gun over Donny's head—

"Stop," said Mary. "Go, Donny. See what you can do for him."

He looked at her. Then he shrugged and stood. Shorty supervised as Donny took Nick by the shoulders and dragged him back into the storage room. Nick groaned once and was silent.

"That's better," said Red.

"He's still alive," said Shorty, through the doorway. "Should I just ...?"

Red shook his head. "Let's not upset our friends here."

He smiled. Like a used car salesman, Mary thought. "See folks, we have to have a little discussion with your pal, Vince. So we're gonna wait quietly until he gets here and then we can leave all you good people in peace."

He raised his hands in a friendly gesture, apparently certain he had won them over. "You understand?"

"We sure do," said Mrs. Swoboda. She pulled out her knitting, never looking away from him. "You know what, sonny? You remind me of my grandson Lionel. Doesn't he remind you of Lionel, Mary?"

"He sure does."

Donny returned. He was wearing only a t-shirt, having shed the jacket in back. Shorty was behind him, gun in hand.

"Welcome back, soldier," said Red. "Take a pew."

He nodded to Shorty. "Go over by the front door, in case Vince shows up. I understand this place is really quiet on Monday nights, but let's lower the lights, just in case. Not dark, but we don't want people seeing guns do we?"

"Where are the lights, gimp?" Shorty asked Cliff.

"Drop dead."

Red shook his head. "Let's not be stupid, okay? You want us to threaten this lady here," he gestured at Mary, "so you can look tough before you give in? I don't think—"

"The lights are on the left side of the pizza oven," said Cliff. He didn't want to meet Mary's eyes. Was he ashamed of being sensible?

Red turned some of the lights out, giving them a better view out than people had in.

"That's better. Whoa, quite a mess there." He was looking at the floor. "You got cleaning stuff?"

"In the back," said Mary.

"Show me."

Red followed her to the storage room. A large, wheeled bucket held the mop and cleaning supplies. Mary pushed it toward the door and then gasped. Nick lay on the floor, his chest covered with Donny's jacket.

Mary left the bucket and walked over to him.

"Let's go," said Red.

"You can wait a minute," she said, and knelt down.

"Listen, sugar—"

She spun to face him. "Maybe you haven't noticed but I'm the one keeping people calm in there. If I start screaming your friend is going to have shoot everyone." Before you intend to.

Red thought about it. He smiled again. "Okay. Take a minute."

Mary nodded. She touched Nick's cheek, which felt hot. His eyes opened. "What happened?"

"You got shot." Donny had tried to use his jacket to stop the bleeding. It seemed to be working.

"By those jokers?" He frowned. "Can't believe it."

"You took the time to get out Mrs. Swoboda out of danger."

"I did?" He sighed. "Town's made me soft."

"I think you're sweet. You need anything?"

His eyes opened wider and he focused on her. "Save Vince."

"We'll try." She patted his arm. "You hang in there."

Mary stood up and nodded to Red. She took hold of the mop and pushed the bucket through the doors into the main room. She saw Cliff let out a breath, and smiled at him.

As she began to mop, Mary forced her mind away from the nature of the mess, trying instead to think about how they could all get out alive.

Shorty stood near the door, watching out the window. Red was leaning at the counter, watching her work.

Any minute now, Mary thought. Any minute now Vince will arrive.

"All done?" said Red, still smiling. "Good. Push the cart to the back door, but don't go through. Now sit down."

"Why are you after Vince?" Cliff asked.

"Shut up," said Shorty, not taking his eyes off the door.

"No, it's okay," said Red. "See, Vince used to run a business back east. He quit because some people didn't like his methods. The guy who took over—"

"Jess," said Donny.

Red did a double-take. "Vince has been chatty, huh? Yeah, Jess is being just as uncooperative as his uncle used to be. Holding back progress. We're hoping Vince can convince him to be more reasonable."

"You call this reasonable?" asked Mrs. Swoboda. "Shooting poor Nick?"

"He shot first," said Red. "Let's all stay calm, okay? As soon as Vince gets here we can settle things."

Shorty chuckled.

When Vince comes, Mary thought, either they kill him to send a message to his nephew, or they kidnap him for the same reason. Either way, they won't leave witnesses alive.

She looked at her fellow witnesses.

Cliff stared back, his face pale and covered with sweat. His hands were pressing on his leg, which must have been in agony.

Mrs. Swoboda, ignoring the whole world, had gone back to work on her latest knitting project, an ugly lump of purple wool.

Donny rocked back and forth, staring at the opposite wall and not seeing it. God, Mary thought, he's back in whatever happened to him in the war.

If anything was going to get done before Vince arrived, it was up to her.

But when would Vince get here? If he didn't come with Nick, he usually arrived when the pizza would be ready.

Then she knew what to do, even before she checked her watch.

"We've got a problem."

Red looked at her. "What?"

"That pizza you ordered."

He looked amused. "You want us to pay for it?"

"It's ready to come out of the oven."

"That's okay. We won't have time to eat it."

"But it's about to burn. In five minutes there'll be so much smoke coming out that none of us will be able to stay, no matter what you do."

Red stared at the big oven and then nodded. "Okay. Take it out."

Cliff started to stand up. "Not you. The lady."

Mary got out of her booth and walked around the counter, close to where Shorty stood. She picked up the wooden peel and opened the oven.

With practiced skill she slid the pizza out and onto a round aluminum tray on the counter. Leaving the peel on the counter, she picked up a pizza cutter and started to slice.

"There's no need for that," said Red. "Sit down."

"Won't take a minute," said Mary. "There. It's not badly burned. Anybody want some?"

She picked up the tray.

"Put it down and come back to the booth," said Red, gesturing with the gun.

"Oh, come on," said Mary cheerfully. "We're probably all hungry. How about you, Donny?"

The young man stared at her blankly.

"Come on," she said. "The first one's free!"

Vince's phrase seemed to awaken something in the young man. He blinked and rose slowly to his feet.

"Sit down, jackass," said Red.

Mrs. Swoboda dropped her knitting on the table and struggled to stand up. "You stop picking on that boy!" she screamed. "Stop picking on him!"

Red was trying to look in all directions at once. Shorty moved closer.

Mary slipped around the counter. She stood on tiptoe and slammed the tray onto Shorty's head, as hard as she could.

Pizza side down.

He let out a yip; suddenly covered with cheese and tomato sauce, all piping hot from the oven.

Donny shot out of his booth, aiming at Red, who dodged. Not slowing down, Donny slammed straight into Shorty.

As the two men grappled, Red stood nearby shouting and trying to figure out how to shoot Donny while staying out of the way of Shorty's waving gun. He never saw Cliff struggling out of his booth. Cliff grabbed the pizza peel and swung it like a baseball bat.

The thin edge hit Red just below the base of his skull. For one horrific moment Mary thought it would take his head clean off.

But of course the wood wasn't sharp enough for that. When the blade struck, Red's head snapped back, his arms flew up, and he crashed face down onto the floor. His gun skittered across the tiles and hit the back wall.

Cliff hobbled after it. Mary hurried to the tumbling brawl in front of the counter. Shorty was on top of Donny and all four of their hands were on the pistol, trying to wrestle it free.

While Mary wondered what to do, Mrs. Swoboda walked calmly up, and rammed a knitting needle into Shorty's elbow. He screamed and let go of the gun, reaching desperately to pull the needle out.

The old lady leaned over him. "If you struggle," she said sweetly, "guess where I'll stick the other one!"

"Get off him," said Cliff. He had Red's gun now.

Shorty scowled and dropped to the floor. Donny, now the sole possessor of the other pistol, scurried to his feet and stood beside Cliff, who nodded. "Call 911. Use the wall phone."

"Nick's gun …"

"I know." He bent over Red, still unconscious, and pulled the pistol from his belt. "Mary, check on Nick."

"Sure," she said. "But first …" She grabbed Cliff and kissed him, hard.

"Wow," said Mrs. Swoboda.

When they broke the clinch Cliff stared at Mary in surprise.

"My hero," she said.

"Yeah?" He grinned.

Nick was unconscious, but still breathing. Mary went back and reported it.

"You people have no idea how much trouble you're in," said Shorty. He still sat on the floor, not far from Red.

"You hush, sonny," said Mrs. Swoboda. "Or I'll stab you again." She waved a knitting needle dramatically. "Pow! Wait until my grandkids hear about this. Boring, am I?"

"You are all dead," said Shorty. "The people who sent us are gonna kill you."

Cliff shook his head. "Shut up and count your blessings."

Shorty stared at him. "How do you figure that?"

"Everyone knows the first guy to talk to the cops gets the best deal." He gestured at Red. "By the time your playmate recovers from his concussion you can blame everything on him, and talk yourself into the witness protection program."

"Yeah?" Shorty thought that one over. "I know a lot. They'll have to give me a hell of a deal."

"No honor among thieves," said Mrs. Swoboda. "Typical."

"Cops and ambulances are on their way," said Donny. "Cliff, you swung that paddle like Barry Bonds."

"I used to play ball in school. Never thought I'd—"

The door opened. Everyone turned to stare at a tough-looking gray-haired man. He looked wide-eyed at the two men on the floor, and the people holding guns.

"My God! What happened here?"

"Come in, Vince," said Mary. "We're just showing some visitors a little Roseville hospitality."

Our second story takes us from Middle America, across the Atlantic, and to the city of Manchester, in England. Pondering on the drunken plans oft made in late night pub sessions, Judy Brownsword pens a tale of three friends caught up in a game of murder.

Fresh from the world of flash fiction, where she has finished first frequently, The Pact is Ms Brownsword's first foray in longer length. We certainly hope it will not be her last.

The Pact

By Judy Brownsword

It started, as these crazy ideas often do, in the pub on a Friday night. Johnny, Julie and me sitting in a bar somewhere in the vicinity of Canal Street. The three of us went way back, we'd met at university during Freshers' week, and hit it off right away.

We made a slightly odd trio. Johnny was the archetypal wild child, rarely attended lectures, always the instigator of any ridiculous undergraduate prank, yet still came through with a respectable 2.1 despite doing almost no work.

Julie worked hard, did all her assignments on time, but nevertheless managed to party all weekend and several nights in the week too. Disgustingly attractive with long chestnut hair and a cheerleader figure, she trailed men behind her wherever she went. I always thought the two of them would get it together and I'd end up getting squeezed out of the group, but amazingly it never happened.

Then there was me, slightly mousy, slightly dull, not particularly academic, but with superb organizational skills. I was the one who would arrange the parties, spot the flaws in Johnny's crazy schemes and figure out how to get around them.

Ten years on, we weren't that different. Johnny was a stockbroker, all smart suits and fast cars and a personal life full of exotic women and soft drugs, although I always suspected there might be something else he wasn't telling even us. Julie ran her own art gallery and I was her assistant, which effectively meant that I ran the place and she gallivanted around the world schmoozing with clients and choosing pieces for the collection.

It had reached the tequila stage of the evening, and we were discussing the major news of the day.

"I don't see the problem," said Julie. "A serial killer is dead. That's a good thing as far as I'm concerned. I don't care if it was suicide. Better than wasting our money on an expensive court case and keeping him in jail for the next 20 years."

"But he died on his own terms! Don't his victims deserve justice?" I replied.

"What justice? They're dead, and now so is he. The world is a better place without him."

Julie set down her glass with an air of finality, sloshing some of the amber liquid over the table as she did so.

"I agree," said Johnny. "Good riddance."

I wasn't sure I agreed, but I knew better than to try to argue my corner once the two of them were in agreement on something, so I just shrugged and signalled to the barman for another round of drinks.

"So," asked Johnny, "If you could rid the world of one person, who would it be?"

"Stan." Julie stated, without hesitation.

Johnny and I both nodded our agreement. Stan had married Julie's mother when Julie was four. Years of systematic abuse had followed until Julie had finally fought back, aged 15. The abuse stopped, but she had never confided in her mother, who was still apparently happily married to Stan. If Julie's mother ever wondered why her daughter always contrived to avoid being in the same room as her husband, she never asked.

"Good choice, Jules," said Johnny. "How about you, Janey?"

"Dunno. I'm not sure there's anyone that I want to get rid of that much."

Julie raised one elegantly shaped eyebrow. "What, really? Not even Ian?"

"Ian? Well, yeah, he was a bastard, but I think bumping him off would be a bit harsh."

"Do you? Have you forgotten your broken collarbone? Not to mention all the bruises you assured us were 'just an accident'?"

I gave a wry smile as I remembered the bizarre sensation of time slowing down as I fell backwards down the stone steps after one of our more heated arguments. It had been the wake up call I needed to leave a brutal bully, after several neighborly calls to the police had failed to change anything.

"No. You're right. Total bastard. We'll add him to the list. Johnny, who's yours?"

"Probably the sod who gave me a parking ticket last week, wish I knew who he was. Perhaps we should just work our way through the city's traffic wardens?"

"Sounds fair to me." I joked, as we poured salt on our hands in preparation for our third tequila.

As we set our glasses down, Julie leaned forward, flushed from the alcohol, and said in a low voice, "You know what? I think we should do it."

"What? Bump off all the traffic wardens?"

"No, idiot." she said, throwing me a contemptuous glance, "I meant Stan and Ian, obviously."

"What!? Don't be ridiculous, you can't go around murdering people just because they did something bad. That's what the justice system is for, remember?"

"Oh, screw the justice system!"

Johnny and I exchanged shocked glances. It's pretty rare to see Julie lose her cool, and even rarer for her to use language stronger than 'damn and blast' when she's particularly annoyed.

"Sorry, Jane." Julie continued. "But honestly, the justice system is impotent to deal with people like Stan and Ian, and you of all people know it."

"Sure, it's not perfect, but that still doesn't give us the right to go around murdering people!"

Julie put her hand on my arm and said urgently, "Listen, Jane. My niece is two years old. My brother doesn't know that there's any reason why 'Grandpa' shouldn't baby-sit. The only way to make sure that he doesn't treat her the way he treated me is to make sure he can't. And as for Ian, just because you got away from him before you were seriously injured doesn't mean that other women will be so lucky."

I had never seen her like this before. There was a fanatical light in her eyes and I barely recognized the Julie I had known for so long. I looked to Johnny for support, but was dismayed to see him thoughtfully scratching his Friday stubble, with a glint in his eye, which I recognised as trouble.

"Oh no. Johnny, tell me you aren't taking this seriously?"

"Well, I was just thinking, providing we make sure it doesn't look like murder, there would be no reason for anyone to suspect us. We're the only ones who know about Stan's little predilections, and Janey, you haven't seen Ian for 2 years, why would anyone think you'd go back and kill him after all this time?"

"But … I … That's not the point!"

"Come on Janey, you know it's the right thing to do. Besides, you know we couldn't do it without you."

I could see I was fighting a losing battle. Knowing what Johnny is like when he gets a bee in his bonnet, I decided to play along, confident that I would be able to talk sense into them in the morning.

"OK, OK! What did you have in mind?"

"Well, let's start with Stan. Jules, does he have a regular routine?"

"He's in The Feathers most nights. That's his local, he stays there until closing time then walks home."

"Right, so we go down there one evening, Janey can lure him into some secluded spot with her fantastic cleavage then I'll jump him and sort him out."

"That is the most ridiculous idea I've ever heard!" I objected. "Firstly, how does beating him to death not look like murder? Secondly, I have actually met the man before, he'd probably recognise me, and thirdly, he's a big bloke, what makes you think you could 'sort him out'? You're more likely to get yourself killed. And fourthly, don't make personal remarks."

"All good points," he conceded. "This is why we need you to come up with a sensible plan."

"Nothing bloody changes," I muttered to myself. "OK, how about a hit and run? It will be late and he'll have been drinking. If we nick a sports car and run him over, the police will think it's a hit and run joyrider, and after a few weeks of looking for witnesses will chalk it up to bad luck."

Johnny's eyes lit up. "Great plan, let's do it!"

"Hold on a second, I don't know how we're going to go about stealing a sports car."

"Don't you worry babes, I can handle that bit".

"Oh, well, that is good news." I reflected that my suspicions about Johnny's darker side hadn't been entirely unfounded.

"Right, so what about Ian? Hit and run again?" asked Johnny.

"Umm, I'm not sure I'm comfortable with that. Someone might make a connection between the two. But I'm not sure how else to make it look like an accident."

"What about an overdose?" asked Julie.

"I'm not sure anyone would buy that. He never seemed the suicidal type to me."

"Honestly Jane, you can be dense sometimes. I meant a recreational drug overdose. Did you never watch 'Pulp Fiction'?"

"Oh, OK," I said, bristling slightly. "I suppose that makes more sense. I guess one of your contacts could provide the necessary?"

"I should think so."

"Right, so how are we going to persuade him to take it?" asked Johnny.

"Oh please," I replied. "After a couple of drinks that guy will take any-thing, especially if a pretty girl offers it to him. That'll be the easy bit, but Julie, I'm afraid that'll have to be you. I don't think I'll be able to convince him!"

"It'll be my pleasure."

"OK, that's sorted then. Johnny to take out Stan and Julie to deal with Ian."

"What about you?" asked Julie. "You can't be the only one not getting your hands dirty."

"But we've only got two victims; I can't just kill someone for the hell of it! No, Johnny, not even a traffic warden."

"Tell you what," said Johnny. "Let's go ahead with these two anyway, then I'll nominate a third, and it'll be Jane's turn."

I wasn't keen on this idea, but agreed to save yet more arguments.

"But you'll have to do it," he pressed me. No ducking out on us if you get cold feet."

"Alright!"

"Good, then let's make it a pact." He raised three fingers in the air in an approximation of the scout salute. "Repeat after me … 'We do solemnly declare …'"

"What? We aren't 12, you know," Julie objected.

"Well, we've got to do something to seal the deal," said Johnny grumpily. "This isn't just some vague notion you know. If we're going to do it, we need to all be in, all the way."

"OK then. Let's drink to it." Julie raised her glass. "Here's to making the world a safer place."

I joined the others in the toast, telling myself that I'd definitely be able to dissuade them from this insane plan in the cold light of day.

"Right," Johnny said as he glanced at his watch. "I'd better get going."

"Why? Where have you got to be?" asked Julie.

"Well, it's 11:15 now. Stan will be walking through the industrial estate at about ten to twelve. That's the perfect spot, 'cos it'll be deserted. That only gives me 35 minutes to find a car and get down there."

"You're planning to do it tonight?" I asked, aghast.

"Sure, why wait?"

"Well, because we need to plan everything to make sure you don't get caught."

"I dunno, if we plan too much, it might become obvious that we'd done it deliberately. I reckon it's best just to wing it."

"Johnny, seriously. Please just let's take some time to make sure we've thought this through!"

He looked at me coldly as he shrugged on his jacket. "No need. I'm going now."

My heart sank.

"Oh God. In that case I'm coming with you. Then at least there'll be two of us to deal with any complications."

"I'll come too," said Julie.

"I don't think that's a good idea. If we do get caught it would be a bit of a coincidence that the victim's stepdaughter was in the car. Why don't you go home and watch some telly. Then you can talk us through what you watched to provide us with an alibi, we can say we were all at your flat all evening. We'll join you when we're done."

"Good thinking, Jane. I'll head off now." And with that, she was gone.

"Are you sure you're up for this?" asked Johnny.

"No, but I'm even more sure you're not doing it on your own."

⸺ ❖ ⸺

We walked briskly through the cold night air, towards the more affluent suburbs where Johnny thought he might have a better chance of finding an appropriate vehicle. I made a few more attempts to get him to delay until another night, but he wasn't having it. After a short while we stopped.

"You keep walking along this road. I'll catch you up shortly," he said as he vanished into the darkness back the way we had just come.

I walked on, shivering, hoping against hope that he wouldn't be able to find a suitable car. Did he really have the wherewithal to steal a car anyway? He never spoke about his life before university, but surely there was nothing that bad in his past? Five minutes later, I heard the low rumble of an outsized exhaust and, turning, saw Johnny pull up beside me at the wheel of a black Mitsubishi.

We arrived earlier than we anticipated at the industrial estate, and parked in the shadows of a long, low warehouse, where we could watch the road without being spotted. The place was eerily deserted, just a few empty ParcelForce vans parked near the loading bay, a sharp contrast to the bustle of the day, when there could be up to 15 of them jostling for position.

We sat there for several minutes in silence, watching the moths fluttering in the sodium light. Then we saw a figure at the other end of the street.

"Is that him?" asked Johnny.

"I'm not sure. It's a long way off."

Johnny glared at me. "Don't mess me about."

I sighed, realizing I was defeated.

"Yes, it's him."

"Right, then let's do this."

I nodded without speaking, and double-checked my seatbelt.

We pulled out of our hiding place and onto the road heading away from Stan. Confused, I glanced across at Johnny.

"Gotta get some speed up. I don't want to get this wrong."

That statement brought home to me, for the first time, exactly what it was we were about to do. I could see Stan in the distance, and hear snatches of song. He clearly didn't have a care in the world.

Johnny turned the car around and we sat there for a few moments, motionless, with Stan in our headlights at a distance. Several seconds went by, and I wondered whether Johnny was having second thoughts.

I was just about to speak when he pressed hard on the accelerator, and we were off. I was pushed back in my seat, heart pounding, gripping my seatbelt with both hands. Time seemed to slow down, and I became acutely aware of the roughness of the seat belt under my fingers, Katrina and the Waves singing "Walking on Sunshine" on the radio, and the sickly smell of the cardboard air freshener shaped like a pine tree hanging from the rear view mirror.

Then we hit him. He was flipped up onto the bonnet, and I saw his head impact the windscreen in front of me, then the glass shattered and I could see no more.

The car skidded to a halt and we both looked back to see the body lying in the road.

"Do you think we need to go back and make sure?" Johnny asked.

"No. He's dead," I said with conviction, remembering the vision of Stan hitting the windscreen. "Let's get out of here."

The rest of the evening is a blur. I remember abandoning the car in a nearby field and setting fire to it. Then the long, cold walk back to Julie's flat, neither of us speaking, Johnny chain-smoking all the way. When she opened the door to let us in, she could tell by our faces that the deed had been done. She didn't ask for details and we didn't volunteer any.

A short piece appeared in the paper the next day, saying that a local man had been killed in a hit and run, and that the police were appealing for witnesses. Julie went to comfort her mother and found her in tears of relief, as Stan had also been abusing her for years, but she'd felt unable to tell anyone.

And that, it appeared, was that. For weeks afterwards, I jumped at every knock on the door, expecting it to be the police. But nothing happened. No negative repercussions at all, it seemed. Even Julie's mum had recovered surprisingly quickly from years of abuse and was dating a charming gentleman, whose apparent worst flaw was a tendency to spend a little too much money on flowers.

I began to feel that maybe what we had done wasn't such a bad thing after all.

A few weeks later, when it seemed that the dust had settled, Johnny brought up the subject of Ian. I protested. I still didn't like the idea of meting out our own justice. I pointed out that the pact and the first murder had occurred under the influence of quite a lot of alcohol, and that we shouldn't let one drunken mistake influence our current actions. We had been lucky to get away with it the first time, and it was asking for trouble to go ahead with our plan. But both Julie and Johnny were adamant, and I knew this was another argument I was destined to lose. When Julie told me one of her friends had seen Ian's current girlfriend on her way to work wearing dark glasses and a much heavier foundation than usual, I finally gave in. The police hadn't been able to help me, but maybe we could help her.

I was sitting in the Gallery, trying to coax a jumble of Julie's notes into some semblance of order when she came in looking pleased with herself.

"I've been thinking about Ian," she announced.

"Rather you than me. Well?"

"Well … a friend of a friend has provided the means. I just need to find a way of administering it. Any idea where he's likely to be this weekend?"

"I can make a couple of educated guesses."

This time, we decided that the three of us would go out. I needed to be there to make a positive identification. Although both Johnny and Julie had met Ian a couple of times, he hadn't really liked to socialize with my friends. Indeed, he hadn't really liked me socializing with my friends either; the reason for my broken collarbone.

To be on the safe side, Julie had gone for a Goth look, which was very different from her usual designer-label persona. I did a double-take myself when she came out of the bathroom wearing a very convincing black wig partnered with blood red lipstick and black nail varnish, and a black PVC corset with matching miniskirt and fishnet tights.

Johnny's jaw nearly hit the ground. "Wow Jules, you look amazing!"

"Give it a rest," Julie replied, clipping him round the ear.

"To be fair, Julie, it is quite a transformation," I said. "But please tell me you haven't really had your nose pierced?"

"No, it's just a stick on. Good though, isn't it?"

"You bet. The tattoo is a nice touch as well."

The Pact

After schlepping around a few of Ian's favorite clubs, we finally found him in The Basement, one of the less salubrious clubs in the city. True to its name, the entrance is down a flight of concrete steps in an uninviting back alley. The walls are also concrete, covered in graffiti-style art, and the dance floor is sticky. Johnny elbowed his way to the bar, while Julie and I made our way to a raised seating area, where I could survey most of the club.

I spotted Ian almost immediately, dancing with a girl almost certainly not old enough to be there, who did not appear to be holding her drink well. I pointed him out to Julie, who immediately went onto the dance floor, and made her way over to where Ian and the young girl were. She started dancing near to Ian, throwing him appraising glances.

It didn't take him long to notice, and soon he started dancing with Julie, clearly thinking that this attractive, confident woman was a better bet than the flagging teenager he had previously had in his sights. She had wandered off, looking tearful, and I was glad to see her leaving with friends.

Glancing over at Ian and Julie, I saw her whispering suggestively in his ear, and then they set off together towards the gents' toilets.

Johnny came over to me with three beer bottles. They cost a fortune, but are the safest thing to drink in a dive like this. "Where's she gone?"

I nodded towards the gents. "We found him."

"Bloody hell, she doesn't mess about, does she?"

"Neither does he."

Johnny laughed at this, then sat down so that, facing him, I could keep an eye on the toilet door. After about 20 minutes, Julie reappeared, alone, and calmly left the club, exchanging a smile and a wink with the bouncers on her way out. Johnny and I finished our drinks and caught up with her on the high street.

"Well?" I asked, "What happened?"

"You were right," she replied.

"About what?"

"After a couple of drinks he'll take anything. He didn't even ask me what it was! He passed out almost immediately. I left him locked in the cubicle, no idea how long it'll be until they find him."

Julie rang me early the next morning. "He's not dead."

"Not dead? How do you know?"

"It was in the paper. He was taken to hospital and is currently in intensive care. He hasn't been named yet, but I'm pretty sure it's him."

"How can that have happened? I thought you said that it was a sure thing?"

"Well, apparently he's got a stronger constitution than we gave him credit for."

"Oh hell. Do you think he'd be able to identify you?"

"I doubt it. He was fairly drunk to start with. Besides, if we're lucky, he won't wake up. We'll just have to sit tight."

"Yeah, I guess."

We heard no more for the next few days, then an old acquaintance phoned me up, a friend of Ian's family. "Did you hear about Ian?"

"No, what about him?" I forced myself to keep my tone light.

"He was taken to hospital a few days ago after an overdose. He was in a coma, but apparently he came round yesterday."

"God, that's awful. Is he going to be OK?"

"Not exactly. He's severely brain damaged, doesn't recognise his family and has limited speech and movement. The doctors say it's unlikely that there'll be much improvement. Look Jane, I'm sorry to be the one to tell you this. I know you'd had your differences, but I thought you ought to know."

Putting the phone down, I realized that I was shaking. I sat down slowly, trying to control the waves of nausea. This was not the way it should have happened. I couldn't stop thinking about the burden on his family, especially his mother, whom I had always rather liked. I couldn't bear the thought of her having to spend the rest of her life looking after him.

In the pub that evening, I tried to explain my feelings to Julie and Johnny.

"What is wrong with you?" asked Julie in amazement. "As far as I'm concerned, it was a complete success. True, things might not have gone to plan, but the idea was to protect innocent people from Stan and Ian, and that's been achieved."

"Yes, but it's one thing to kill someone quickly, another to turn them into a vegetable."

"Can't see that we made much difference in Ian's case."

"Johnny, that's not funny!" I turned on him. "I can't believe we ever started this. I want nothing more to do with this stupid pact."

I stood up to leave, but he grabbed me by the wrist.

"Don't think you can quit now. We had an agreement."

Julie nodded.

"Let go of me, you're hurting!"

"I mean it, Jane. We're in this together, all the way."

I shook my wrist free and walked out, blinking back the tears.

There was a certain coldness between us after that, but the topic wasn't raised again, and I began to think that they'd seen the sense in what I had said and that they wouldn't identify a final victim.

I should have known better.

It was almost a year later when Johnny announced, "I've found our last victim."

My heart sank, but I was prepared to hear him out. Time had assuaged some of my guilt over Ian, and I knew that if Johnny was going to get this bee in his bonnet again, my life wouldn't be worth living if I didn't see it through. And, after all, the principle of making the world a safer place was still sound.

"Go on."

"Read this."

Johnny handed me a newspaper cutting. It was just a few lines long, reporting that a local councillor had been cleared of causing death by dangerous driving following an accident in which three people had been killed. I looked at Johnny, confused.

"You want me to kill this guy? Why?"

"I've been following this case, it's not as straightforward as this report would have you believe. He didn't stop at a red light, refused to take a breathalyzer test, and he had three previous convictions for drunk-driving. He should have been locked up for murder, and he doesn't even get convicted of death by dangerous driving! I'm telling you Janey, there's something dodgy going on."

"Well, OK, I admit it looks suspicious, but you don't actually know this guy, do you?"

"Not personally. What's your point?"

"Well, we knew Stan and Ian, we had first-hand evidence of what they were capable of. I can't kill someone just because of a bunch of newspaper reports. If he was acquitted, perhaps the accident wasn't his fault."

"Oh, for God's sake," Johnny snapped, "I've been though all the reports, there's definitely some sort of cover up going on."

"Well, if you say so, but why are you so interested in this particular case? There must be loads of drunk drivers who kill people and get away with it."

Johnny looked a bit sheepish. "Well, he has particular responsibility for traffic in the city …"

"Oh my God. You actually want me to bump off the head of traffic wardens! Tell me you're kidding."

"Don't try to wriggle out of this. We had an agreement."

"Well, I know we did, but this is completely different, can't you see that? Julie, what do you think?"

Julie shrugged. "We agreed that Johnny would select the third person."

I opened my mouth to argue my case further, but saw the look on Johnny's face and sighed instead. "If I do this, is that it? No more stupid pact stuff?"

"Janey, I promise."

"OK, you win. Let me do some research into this guy and come up with a plan, then we can meet to discuss it. Johnny, how about your flat next Saturday?"

"It's a date."

That week, I dug out all the newspaper cuttings I could find on the trial, and put these into a folder with other information I had managed to uncover about the man and his likely movements. On Saturday, I arrived at Johnny's flat with a bundle of papers under my arm.

"Hey babes, wow, you have been busy!" He said as he opened the door.

"Well, you know me. I don't like to do things by halves. Why don't you start looking through this lot while I go and put the kettle on?"

"Yeah, alright." He took the bundle through to the living room, where Julie was already sitting.

I went into the kitchen, filled the kettle and put it on the gas hob. Johnny has never been tidy, so I washed up three mugs to use while waiting for the kettle to boil. When I arrived in the living room with the coffees, they were deep in discussion.

"Hey Janey, we've been through this lot. Did you have any bright ideas about how to do this?"

"No, not really. It's going to be much harder, and more dangerous than the other two, 'cos we haven't got the inside info this time. Johnny, are you sure you wouldn't rather wait to find someone more suitable?"

Johnny glared at me. "Don't start that again."

"OK, OK." I held up by hands in a conciliatory fashion. "I just wanted to make sure you wouldn't change your mind."

"I won't, so let's get on."

Johnny reached for his cigarettes. "Could you not light up just yet?" I asked him. "I can't concentrate if you're smoking."

We thrashed around a few ideas, but the publicity surrounding our victim made most plans too risky. He was infamous for being at the centre of several council corruption scandals. In fact, we probably weren't the only ones plotting against him.

"We could just let someone else kill him." I said brightly. Johnny wasn't amused.

Eventually, even Johnny agreed that more research was needed, and we made arrangements to meet the following weekend.

"See you Saturday then." I said as I left the flat.

I jogged down the steps onto the street and set off down the street at a brisk pace. I had gone about 200 yards when I heard the explosion as Johnny's cigarette ignited the gas I had left on in the kitchen. I heaved a sigh of relief, and walked away.

━━━◆◆◆━━━

Let's lighten things up a bit with our next story. The annual pie contest at the Patoula County Fair is under way, but beneath all that sugary sweetness, ill feelings ferment foul flavor. "Sweet Murder" conjures up a small town whose inhabitants, and their names, fall squarely in the quirky side of town.

A photographer as well, Ms Jones also writes in the field of magical realism, but a life-long love for mysteries keeps her well rooted in our genre.

Sweet Murder

by Magdalena Jones

Morris Beady rubbed the back of his neck and adjusted his string tie. He pulled his watch out of his pocket, glanced at it, and raised his eyes heavenward in silent prayer. Then he thrust his way through the back flaps of the white canvas tent and mounted the podium. He ducked his head once and said "Good afternoon, ladies," in the fine baritone that was heard every Sunday morning on Glory Salvation Radio and every July as emcee of the Patoula County Fair. His voice stood him in its usual good stead. It did not belie the utter trepidation that overtook him at the sight of all those flowered hats, embroidered white hankies and gimlet eyes.

"Well, it's a fine day at the Patoula County Fair, now isn't it, ladies?" said Mr. Beady.

The powdered faces before him were grim despite the dappled July sun dancing outside, the heart-entrancing sound of the calliope and the rich aroma of spice, fruit and melt-in-your-mouth chocolate filling the tent.

"Ahem, well," said Mr. Beady. This would not be the year when the gentlewomen of Patoula City would finally reach across the aisle to one another in sisterly unity, he could see that already. The middle aisle might well be the great wall of China instead of a swath of beaten down grass. Mr. Beady knew every lady in his audience, could have recited in his sleep on which side of the aisle he'd find them too.

"I shall not keep you in suspense any longer," said Mr. Beady, really meaning he was trying to keep his own torture as short as possible, "Our first finalist is … Weezy Ann Witherspoon!"

The left side of the aisle broke out in frenzied applause. A tiny woman in a hat laden with bunches of cherries rose, smoothed out her dress and walked up to the podium. On the right side of the aisle the hankies grew agitated, covered pursed mouths, dabbed at eyes, fluttered in annoyance. Mr. Beady didn't know why. Weezy Ann Witherspoon had been a finalist every year for the past couple of decades or so.

It was tradition in Patoula County for the finalists in the pie contest to give a little speech. Mr. Beady retreated to a folding chair and gazed at his hands.

Weezy Ann Witherspoon trotted up to the podium with a vigor that defied her apparent years, due to the dexterity she had accumulated over thirty years of harvesting fruits from her orchard faster than any of her mere male farmhands.

"Thank you, Mr. Beady, for this great honor," said Weezy Ann Witherspoon. "My pie this year is the cradle of two magnificent fruits: the first is from the great cherry tree, the fruit of which will always be synonymous with General George Washington; the second is that most amiable, succulent, tasty and fragrant of all fruits, the fruit that is heralded above all others, the humble yet noble apple. The sun-kissed apple and the rich red cherry, my friends: what could be more truly all-American a pie than this? The fruit harvested from the great good earth, born of and giving of the seeds of this great nation, bearing sweetness and color within their very essence. Real pie, my friends, has at its heart fruit, and only fruit."

With this came a venomous glance to the right side of the aisle. Mr. Beady shifted in his chair. "I trust, dear friends, that you shall remember this in your final vote - a vote for the only pie that is a true pie, fruit pie."

Weezy Ann nodded graciously to the left which had risen as one with reedy cheers hissing from each wrinkled throat.

Mr. Beady stepped back to the podium. "Now, for our second finalist! I give you Miss Ida March Popplewell!" The right side of the aisle erupted, the left subsiding immediately into their chairs with a hiss and pointed turning of heads away from the next diminutive figure to mount the podium that day. Ida March Popplewell could have been Weezy Ann Witherspoon's twin but for an unfortunate predilection for ruffles, which extended to the pink hat perched on top of her blue-gray hair.

Ida March Popplewell curtsied to the right side of the tent and clasped her white-gloved hands together. The white gloves hid the wiry tendons in those hands, preternaturally strong after a life spent milking her herd of dairy cows.

"Thank you ever so, Mr. Beady. You must forgive my flutters at this achievement." Mr. Beady didn't know why. Ida March Popplewell was always the other finalist in the Patoula County Fair Pie Contest.

"I have entitled my entry this year the Ever-So-Silky Chocolate Dream Pie—oh! Now you know I meant cream pie," Ida March Popplewell simpered a little over her joke, "My very best prize cows each contributed a pint to this year's pie, my dearest Lucinda and Lolita. There is nothing, dear ladies, like a pie that comes from the warmth of a living creature, born of love that only a cow can give, each mouthful a melting bite of heaven. And if God didn't love us, would he have given us chocolate? He does, and He did. The marriage of two of God's most heavenly gifts come together in my Ever-So-Silky Chocolate Cream Pie. This pie," Here Ida March Popplewell sent a death ray glance at Weezy Ann Witherspoon, "transcends one of mere earth. This pie is nothing less than from the hand of God Hisself. Dear ladies, it humbles me to say so, but a vote for my pie is the only true vote for God."

Ida March Popplewell flounced back to her seat. Mr. Beady got reluctantly to his feet again. It was time for the vote, but he never did have to count. He didn't know how it was that the scheming, bribing, and blackmailing of the two enemy forces always resulted in an equal number of votes for each side, but each and every year that was what happened. Thus every year, Mr. Beady, as master of ceremonies, had to break the tie. Lesser men, he thought, ran from the challenge. Mr. Beady's vest expanded every so slightly each year when he, and only he, stepped up to the challenge. Never mind that every year half of Patoula City turned their noses up at him, boycotted his radio program and didn't buy a single gravestone from him. He, Morris Beady, was the Lion of Patula City.

Peace of a kind did descend during the twenty-four hours the bylaws of the pie contest dictated as the grace period given to resolve a tie. Mr. Beady enjoyed that one single God-given day, enjoyed it to the hilt. For every hour until his universally known bedtime of ten p.m. (Mrs. Beady having laid down the law when a set of blackberry buttermilk cream puffs landed on her great-grandmother's quilt instead of in Mr. Beady's wide open and snoring mouth at two a.m.) Mr. Beady was courted by every female in town.

Making his way home from the fair itself took some little while, Mr. Beady being waylaid by every dimple and simper it was possible for each side to muster, and Mr. Beady, gentleman that he was, seeing it as his duty to be punctilious in his return of such compliments.

This was merely one battlefield however. Weezy Ann Witherspoon and Ida March Popplewell continued their war on Mr. Beady's homefront as well. The unwritten accord was that the Witherspoon contingent might occupy Mr. Beady between Hyacinth and Foxglove Streets, the Popplewell troops were allowed Hemlock to Oleander. Whichever side was engaged on the flirtation front, sorties of combatants on the other would convey salvos of sugary edibles to his door, which Mrs. Beady simply left open so she could get on with her laundry. The dining room table, as a result, greeted Mr. Beady on his return by groaning under the weight of these offerings.

As soon as Mr. Beady arrived home, he hung his white Panama Hat on its wrought iron hook, then proceeded to the dining room. He then took a white linen napkin from the sideboard, tucked it under his chin and sat down before his personal cornucopia of delights. He grabbed a fork and dug in.

In vain did Mrs. Beady urge upon him skinless chicken laced with a light touch of fresh garden thyme with a squeeze of lemon, accompanied by tender peas barely blanched, peas she herself shelled from pods she hand-selected and clipped from their stems.

Mr. Beady, however, could not be moved from the law he lived by. He would eat no sweet the rest of the year, but on this one day, this one glorious, gluttonous day, Mr. Beady ate naught but sweet. Never mind that his stomach became a storm-tossed ship in a typhoon by morning. Mr. Beady considered this peanuts to pay for the wallow in his private plethora of confections.

Mrs. Beady's protestations fell on the deaf ears of Mr. Beady, the ear canals of whom she reckoned were stuffed with the cakes, cookies, and cobblers which had found their way there on account of there being no room left in his stomach.

Upon the following morning, it was invariably and unsurprisingly Mr. Beady's habit to consume only weak tea dosed heavily with Mrs. Beady's own Medicinal Miracle Marvel Honey, known throughout Patoula City as a cure for every ill associated with gastrointestinal distress. (The Fraternal Knights of the Blue Hound kept a large stock on hand down at the Lodge.) Thus fortified, Mr. Beady was ready to face the sinister sea of stiffly quivering flower-bedecked hats awaiting him and his weighty verdict in the white canvas tent at high noon.

Now, truth be told (and you may be shocked to hear this), Mr. Beady's decision was rarely if ever made on the basis of the quality of the two pies brought before him for judgment. No, Patoula City was a small town, a town where folks pretty much knew the other's business, even if they didn't speak in public.

Mr. Beady, merchant that he was, had a fair idea of which contingent, Witherspoon or Popplewell, would yield the most revenue for him in the coming year. He kept a keen ear tuned for that topic most engrossing to many past the prime of life, that is, the health of themselves, their kin, and any passing stranger. He could extrapolate, predicated on his years of experience, who in Patoula City and its environs was most likely to pass on to their great reward in the near future, and tally on the tote board in his mind which faction had the most population with one foot in the grave and therefore more in need of his gravestones.

As far as Mr. Beady was concerned, this score was the only one that counted. Mr. Beady, in fact, knew which way he would vote even before the official tabulation at the pie contest began. He found it entertaining that neither side had ever perceived the reason in his rhyme.

As Mr. Beady surveyed his audience, leaning on his cane (which he'd taken to bringing since the Riot of '08). In his mind he still idly wondered if Weezy Ann Witherspoon's great Uncle Cyril's continued three-pack-a-day habit and worsening cough outweighed Ida Mae Popplewell's second-cousin-once-removed's dementia, but was still pretty certain which one would greet their Maker first.

Mr. Beady held up one hand, and the tent went instantly silent. All eyes on him, Mr. Beady held this precious moment of power a beat longer. He bowed his head (in better form, he knew, than Deacon Fotheringill at Patoula Evangelical Baptist), but just as he was forming the first sonorous syllable, his mouth began to burn.

Was the searing flame that was his tongue God's retribution because he intended to announce the name of one contestant even though this year the other's crust was just a tad more flaky, her choice of filling a mite more sublime? Nonsense, Mr. Beady thought, as sweat rolled down his face. His mind was clear—which was why he didn't understand why his stomach had begun to roll around like a dog in a briar patch.

Was it some recurrence of this morning's tempest? It was true Mrs. Beady's Medicinal Miracle Marvel Honey hadn't achieved its usual standards of stomach-calming, but it had subsided to a dull roar. The roar was now making the Lion of Patula City bilious. The hand that tried to retrieve the Mrs. Beady-embroidered handkerchief residing in his left hand pocket seemed to miss his crisp white jacket altogether. The last thing he saw as his eyes went dark were the expressions on Weezy Ann Witherspoon's and Ida March Popplewell's faces, compounded of praying mantis and crocodile deprived of their prey.

Sheriff Sweetwater brought the news of Mr. Beady's collapse home to Mrs. Beady, from whose hands the plate that had held Weezy Ann's Raspberry Bourbon Balls with Honey Hard Sauce clattered onto the china cake stand that had held Ida March's Triple Layer Sour Cream and Ginseng Surprise Cake. Both shattered onto the heretofore-spotless linoleum floor. Mrs. Beady, who never had accidentally dropped a plate in her life, buried her face in a dish towel and wailed. Sheriff Sweetwater was grateful for the muffling effect of the cloth, and could only awkwardly pat Mrs. Beady's shaking shoulders.

"It was the pie contest killed him!" Mrs. Beady said, one reddened eye peeping out from the merrily flowered fabric. "Those women! They killed my Morris!"

"Now, now, Mrs. Beady," Sheriff Sweetwater said, "Dr. Janey said it was an attack brought on by—"

"The shameless barrage of sweet poison lobbed at my poor Morris' constitution! Why just three months ago, Morris was in to see Doc Cates, and he said Morris' blood pressure was the lowest he'd ever seen! You just ask him!"

Sheriff Sweetwater sighed. He could take the drunken brawls of the town alcoholic, he could handle the hijinks of spirited young men who took it as a personal challenge to paint untoward remarks on the town water tower, and he could even endure the constant bait and switch tactics of the local moonshiners. The sobs of newly made widows unmanned, not to say unsheriffed him.

He could only be relieved when Mrs. Hawkins from next door, who had gotten the news from the usual sources, came over to attend Mrs. Beady, silently gladdened that she was far better attired in her black serge with the white lace collar than Mrs. Beady was in her yellow housedress. She gave the sheriff a sniff that said he was a useless man and he could go now while she took over the fussing. He used his flashing red lights to maneuver through the throng of cars now clogging the road from town.

It was only later on that evening, sitting at home with his wife and grandmother after his children had said their prayers and gone off to sleep, that the tiniest hint of doubt entered his mind. Something was trying to poke through and make itself remembered. Since Sheriff Atwater often found his mind clarified after ruminating with his womenfolk, he folded his hands and cleared his throat.

"What is it, Grandson?" asked his grandmother, as his wife came to sit at the table with them.

"Grandmother, I am like a mole burrowing through darkness for something, something that I know I should bring to the case of the death of Mr. Morris Beady today."

The women nodded their heads crowned with braided hair, one gray shot with black, the other black shot with gray. Of course they knew of Mr. Beady's demise, having heard more eyewitness reports than Sheriff Sweetwater had over fences, sweet tea and much waving of handkerchiefs. They already knew what he should remember, as women do, but waited with patience for him to arrive at his destination or finally ask those who knew how to get there.

"Mr. Beady collapsed at the pie judging today."

The ladies nodded.

"The whole of the town knows Morris Beady ate enough sugar for an entire year in one day, of his own free will. Why should my mind then be poking at this like a dog in a gopher field?"

The ladies waited.

"Doc Janey took one look and said heart attack. Mabel Beady claims Doc Cates said Morris Beady had the lowest blood pressure of any man he knew."

The ladies raised their eyebrows.

"Morris Beady … I was there when he collapsed—just in case anyone had any ideas about repeating the Riot of '08."

The ladies bent forward now.

"His eyes went wide and he near split his mouth open to stick his tongue out, as though it was too fiery to touch any other part of him. Man could have been his own hot springs the way the sweat ran down. His arms flailed, he clutched his chest. He fell down. His whole body rocked with spasms. Seemed as though he was trying to spit something out and couldn't."

His grandmother gave a glance at his wife who quirked up one side of her mouth.

"Great-Aunt Rosella," his wife said.

"Mad honey," said his grandmother.

The ladies waited, as they did with the children, for the sheriff to discover the obvious conclusion they had already arrived at for himself.

Sheriff Beady lifted his face from his hands. His brow cleared. "Wonder if Mrs. Beady still has those plates?" he said, and left the house.

The sheriff had to walk a good quarter mile to get to the Beady house, having decided it was the better part of sheriffing to park instead of block the road. When he opened the back screen door to the kitchen, having determined he couldn't enter the living room without stepping on a feminine toe, he saw that the kitchen table was full of casseroles, the sight of which he approved.

Two women, Mrs. Spurlock and Mrs. Souder were making coffee, while Mrs. Morrissey and Mrs. Mooney were filling a plate of the best china with the choicest selections from the tributes. This would not have astounded the good sheriff so much had he not known for a fact that Mrs. Spurlock and Mrs. Mooney had been established supporters of Weezy Ann Witherspoon for a coon's age and Mrs. Sounder and Mrs. Morrissey staunch lieutenants in Ida March Popplewell's ranks for just as long. He hardly dared breathe as he tipped his hat and shuffled through the kitchen lest he break this wholly unanticipated truce.

"Mrs. Beady," he said, finding her as the one spot of yellow in a covey of black and grey pigeons, "I wonder if I might have just one quiet word, ma'am."

The pigeons parted. Mrs. Beady stepped to the kitchen door.

"Mrs. Beady," the sheriff whispered so none could hear though all strained every hair in their earlobes to try, "do you by any faint chance still have those dishes of Miz Witherspoon's and Miz Popplewell's?"

Mrs. Beady clapped her hands to her mouth and stared at the sheriff. "Well, I washed—"

The sheriff closed his eyes.

"I washed everything but those two. You might recall that when you told me the news I broke those exact two dishes in my distress? I believe they were placed in the waste bin."

The sheriff opened his eyes. He went out the back door to Mrs. Beady's trash bin. There, miraculously unwashed, with traces still of their once-contents, were the Popplewell cake stand and the Witherspoon plate. The sheriff went to borrow a pair of Mrs. Beady's kitchen gloves and two fresh trash bags. He then returned to the trash bin where he carefully picked up every piece of the broken china he could find and bagged them.

One month later, the Patoula County District Attorney brought to trial Weezy Ann Witherspoon and Ida March Popplewell for the murder of Mr. Horace Beady. When it came time to choose twelve of their peers, their respective lawyers at first attempted to negotiate that half the jurors come from the Witherspoon faction and the other half from the Popplewell adherents, but the arrests of their leaders seemed to be the antidote to the spell that had bound said peers unquestioningly to their chosen side. The lawyers found no one who claimed allegiance to either lady, which in turn brought home to them that their clients might be railroaded though in a very genteel way.

The crowning moment of the trial, however, was the testimony by the majestic Mr. Trumbull from the laboratory in the state capitol who stated unequivocally that he'd found traces of the poison grayanotoxin in the honey that had hitherto been the secret ingredient of both defendants' recipes.

Mr. Trumbull, whose deep bass voice and bristling mane of gray hair ensured that all listening believed every word he said, noted that the poison-imbued honey found in both ladies' concoctions was of a strangely concentrated and therefore highly suspicious amount. He delivered a devastating blow to the defendants' vehement denials that they would ever work together on anything, by pronouncing that one dessert made of the toxic honey would not have killed Mr. Beady. Only the double dose of the honey, found in traces on both the cake stand and the plate, added up to the lethal amount.

After which, Sheriff Atwater modestly took the stand to tell of his exploits in the field, during which he found a beehive nestled in the thicket of mountain laurel and rhododendron that the supposed enemies kept so dense as to be almost impenetrable between their two adjoining properties.

The suspect beehive was stripped of its honeycomb, but the sheriff was able to preserve the evidence of mortally poisoned bees and traces of honey, which, it so happened, was identical to that which was used by the defendants in their respective desserts delivered to Mr. Beady's house. (Mr. Trumbull nodded gravely.)

The beehive, the sheriff said, sat directly on the boundary stones set by the defendants' great grandaddies a hundred years ago, with a new-made path extending to each defendant's backyard. He then cited another irreproachable source, the National Geographic Magazine of '88 (Honey Hunters of the Himalayas), which clearly instructed its readers that honey produced from rhododendron and mountain laurel would inevitably contain large amounts of grayanotoxin poison.

Not only was this fact established by National Geographic, but the sheriff testified that "mad honey" had also caused the death of his Great-Aunt Rosella. (The judge had to bang his gravel for an entire minute to shush the titters in his courtroom.)

Not one juror dared withstand the twin profundities of Mr. Trumbull and the National Geographic Magazine, to which every member of the community subscribed. Weezy Ann Witherspoon and Ida March Popplewell were sentenced to life in adjoining cells.

In Patoula City, long-estranged cousins embraced. Tea parties welcoming previous adversaries flourished.

The next year, Mrs. Beady, in resplendent lavender, was awarded the prize for the best pie at the Patoula County Fair. It was universally acknowledged that Mr. Beady had been cognizant of his wife's hitherto unknown prowess in pie-making, which was why she had never been able to enter the pie contest previously, Mr. Beady not wanting to appear swayed by obvious partisanship.

Sheriff Sweetwater was re-elected unanimously, being admired by all for his prowess in finding the well-hidden evidence of the beehive. Although, it must be said, there were a few things the good sheriff missed (which perhaps he might not have if he'd told his grandmother and wife more of his interview with Mrs. Beady): notably the small plaque Mrs. Beady put up amongst her own beehives commemorating the sacrifice that their brothers (and one sister) had made on her behalf; and the onion juice-soaked flowered dish towel that Mrs. Beady had held to her face on hearing the news of her husband's demise, as Mrs. Beady put it through the washing twice, with baking soda and vinegar, before placing it lovingly back in the drawer with its mates.

Time now for a traditional private investigator story, and Herschel Cozine's "The Photograph" certainly fits the bill. Greed, sex, corruption, all part of a day's work for PI Frank Marcus.

Mr. Cozine is well and widely published. His work has appeared in Ellery Queen's Mystery Magazine, Alfred Hitchcock's Mystery Magazine, Mysterical-E, Sherlock Holmes Magazine, and Woman's World. His story, "A Private Hanging" was a finalist for the Derringer award. His latest book, "The Osgood Casebook", is published by Untreed Reads.

The Photograph

by Herschel Cozine

Murder is not my specialty. I have an aversion to violence and blood, and murders usually involve both. As a private investigator, I spend my working hours sitting in a cramped car drinking cold coffee from a Styrofoam cup. I know the location of every motel between here and the Canadian border. It's mind numbing, boring to the point of agony. But it's a living. There are precious few opportunities in this country for a high school dropout.

Of course, if someone other than a wronged spouse wants me to work for him I will jump at the chance. Even an unpleasant murder would be a welcome change.

That change appeared in my doorway looking for all the world like an overgrown Munchkin trying to find his way back to Oz. I was in the process of brewing a fresh pot of coffee when the door opened and he sidled through, looking as if he was entering the principal's office for detention.

He was a small man, no more than five foot four, with a head slightly too large for his body, further accentuated by a flock of red hair that stood out in crazy angles. Horn rimmed glasses that had gone out of style with Buddy Holly, perched on his frail nose.

"Mister Marcus?" he asked in a voice that could only be described as timid.

"You're looking at him," I said. "I was just making some coffee. Would you like some?"

He shook his head, looked around the small room with no apparent purpose in mind, then turned his attention back to me. I motioned to the overstuffed chair and silently invited him to sit down.

"How can I help you?" I asked, taking a sip of coffee, black, with a dash of sugar.

"My name is Brent," he started. "Howard Brent. I'm an attorney."

I acknowledged this bit of information with a lift of an eyebrow, leaned back and waited for him to go on. Instead he studied a spot on the floor—which one I don't know. (My personal favorite is the one that resembles Alfred Hitchcock's profile, but there are many to choose from). I don't have a janitorial service, and housekeeping is not part of my job description.

Finally, shifting his gaze to meet mine, he spoke. "I've been robbed."

He sounded like a Chicago Cubs fan. I refrained from comment and waited for him to continue.

He didn't. I leaned forward and rested my elbows on the desk.

"Sorry to hear that. How can I help you?"

He studied my face with an air of bewilderment, evidently decided that I was trustworthy, and relaxed.

"I need someone to find out who broke into my office, and why."

"That's a job for the police," I said.

"The police aren't involved."

"You didn't notify the authorities?" I asked. "Why not?"

He heaved a sigh and brushed a tangle of hair from his eyes.

"Police are useless in cases like this. No witnesses. No motive. And as far as I can tell, nothing is missing."

"I see," I said. "So in reality you haven't been robbed. It was a break-in."

He nodded. "I guess so."

"Still a crime. The police should be notified."

He shook his head. "No. That's why I'm here. I don't want to deal with them."

He removed his glasses and pinched the bridge of his nose. "In my profession you develop an adversarial relationship with the police."

I started to say something, but he held up his hand. "Don't get me wrong. I'm sure they would investigate, perhaps even apprehend the person who did this. But there are too many confidential matters involved. I don't want them compromised over a break-in that didn't result in any loss."

He sounded as though he were pleading a case to a jury. Force of habit, I suppose. I waited for him to finish, ask me to find his client "not guilty", and rest his case.

Apparently, that had already happened. He sat back in the chair and folded his hands in his lap.

"Defense lawyer?" I asked.

"I beg your pardon?"

"You. You are a defense lawyer, right?"

He gave a tentative nod.

"I deal in civil cases for the most part. But I have handled a few criminal cases. Minor ones. Petty theft. Shoplifting." He paused and reddened. "Prostitution."

I smiled inwardly at the image of him, short and nerdy, seated at the defense table with a prostitute, whispering in her ear, and defending her right to make a living.

"Where did the break-in occur?" I asked.

"My office," Brent said. "Up until last month I had a partner. Well, not really a partner so much as a co-tenant. We shared the office for financial reasons. We didn't collaborate on cases, except to quote precedents and general law matters. He was a divorce attorney."

"What happened to him?"

Brent shifted uneasily in his chair. "He died."

"I'm sorry," I said. "What was the cause?"

"A bullet."

I whistled softly and leaned back in my chair. I wasn't expecting the answer, and was a little taken aback by the monotone in Brent's voice, not at all in keeping with the message.

"Murder?"

He nodded and scratched his nose.

"Did they catch the killer?"

"They have a suspect in custody."

"Who?"

"Milton South," Brent said. "One of William's clients. Or more correctly, ex-client"

"William?"

"William Kenwood. My associate."

I recalled having read of a prominent attorney who had been shot by a former client. "Prominent" is a word greatly overused in the news, and is reserved for certain professions: lawyers, doctors, bank presidents. Have you ever heard of a prominent plumber? As for William Kenwood, I had never heard of the man before he was shot. His death suddenly made him prominent.

I hadn't followed the case other than to note that the suspect had been unhappy with the outcome of his divorce, and blamed Kenwood for the loss of his home to his ex-wife, along with an expensive alimony. Reason enough to commit murder if one cares about that sort of thing.

"How solid is the case against South?" I asked.

Brent shrugged. "I don't know. He is protesting his innocence, of course."

"Are you his lawyer?"

"No. That would be a conflict of interest. Besides, I don't have the credentials for a case of that nature."

I changed the subject.

"Would the break-in have anything to do with Kenwood's death?" I asked.

Brent shrugged. "I don't know." He lowered his head and studied another spot on the rug, or maybe it was the same one he had studied earlier.

"Most of the trashing of the office was William's file cabinet. A lot of his folders were spread around. But some of mine were as well." He raised his eyes. "But all this is conjecture. Would you be willing to look into it?"

This wouldn't be easy. Without a police investigation there would be no record of fingerprints or other pertinent evidence. But if it was easy there would be no need of a private eye and I'd be sweeping streets for a living.

"If, as you say, nothing was taken, then I have to assume it was vandalism." I shook my head. "No motive, no suspects."

Brent's mouth turned downward in a pout and he shrugged his shoulders.

"There is someone out there who has violated my space. I'd sleep better knowing who it is."

I felt a surge of sympathy for the little man. I didn't know how much good I could do for his sleep disorder, but I was in no position to turn down work. Still, I hesitated.

"You haven't given me much to go on. A break-in with nothing taken. No witnesses. No police report." I emphasized the last remark with a scowl. "Is there anyone you know who may have had a reason to do this?"

He shook his head. "No. It's possible that William had dealings with someone who wanted his file. Divorce proceedings can get messy, you know."

"Was Kenwood shady?"

"No," he said, a little too quickly. He sat back in the chair. "No. William Kenwood was a respected attorney."

"Still he was murdered, supposedly for the way he handled a case."

"Not even a respected attorney can please everyone. Especially in a divorce case where feelings run high. At best, only one of the litigants is going to be happy with the outcome."

"Do you have a list of Kenwood's clients?"

"Yes."

"And the files?"

Brent shook his head. "Except for the ones that have been transferred to other attorneys or given to the clients, they are all there in Kenwood's cabinet."

"One hundred an hour plus expenses," I said.

"What?"

"My fee. A thousand retainer. Acceptable?"

Brent considered a moment, his eyes doing a dance across my face. Then silently he took out his checkbook and started to write.

———

"Are you crazy?" Marge frowned at me as she stirred sugar into her coffee.

"No."

She took a sip of coffee, made a face and reached for another packet of sugar.

"Frank, this isn't your line. You aren't a criminal investigator. Unless infidelity is a crime in this state."

"Marge, I hate what I do. Sitting in a cold car outside a second rate motel is not my idea of a good time. It's boring. It's—"

"Hey," she said. "You tailed the Dean of History at the university and caught him boffing the mayor's wife. Now that's OK in my book."

"First of all," I said as I motioned to the waiter for a refill, "I didn't 'catch' him. I sat outside the motel while they did their thing behind closed doors. I can only assume that they were fooling around."

"Ha!" Marge laughed derisively. "They were playing Yahtzee, I suppose. And it wasn't a second rate motel. It was the Saddle Mountain, four stars in the AAA guidebook."

"A lot of good that did," I said. "I was still sitting in my cold cramped 1998 Ford." I leaned forward and put my elbows on the table, mainly to annoy Marge who was a stickler for table manners. She ignored the gesture.

"Well, it's your life," she said.

"Thank you for understanding," I said.

"You're welcome. So where do you go from here?"

"I don't know. Brent hasn't given me anything to go on. I have a meeting with him tomorrow morning."

"That should be a big help. Maybe the guy who did this is hiding in the broom closet."

"What makes you think it's a guy?"

Marge waved a hand. "Guy. Gal. Whatever."

"You don't have much faith in me, do you?"

Marge chuckled and patted my arm affectionately. "Sorry. I really hope you find the guy. Or gal," she said, emphasizing the last word. "It's just that you don't have any information that can help. You said so yourself." She pulled her hand away and glared at my elbows. I sat up straight.

"Well, be that as it may, I'm getting paid—and handsomely I might add—to find the guy, or guys, or guys and gals …"

Marge leaned forward. "Okay. Okay. You've covered all the bases. Good luck."

She stood up, fished in her purse for money. I reached up and snapped it shut.

"My treat."

Marge didn't argue. It was a ritual we went through every time we had lunch together. She smiled warmly, kissed me on the forehead and turned to the door.

"Gotta run," she said. "See you tonight?"

"Seven."

"Don't be late," she said over her shoulders. Another ritual. We had a standing date on Mondays and always at seven. We were becoming too predictable.

The small frame building in the better part of town housed several businesses. An insurance agent, a CPA, and the law offices of Howard Brent and William Kenwood.

Unassuming, yet freshly painted, well landscaped and shaded by an ancient oak, it gave an air of respectability that was necessary for the tenants to have for a successful business. I parked my car in front of the building and killed the engine.

It was a clear, cool midmorning. I could hear the chirping of birds over the traffic as they cooed, courted and dirtied the sidewalk. There was little foot traffic in this part of town. Even though it was zoned for business, it had a residential feel to it, and there was little to bring one to this part of town unless they were looking for a lawyer or insurance.

Brent greeted me as I walked into his office. I looked around, impressed by the brightness and the lack of clutter. And there were no spots on the rug. Either his clients didn't drink coffee or he had a cleaning service.

He motioned me to a leather chair facing his desk. I sat down, leaned back and crossed my legs. Lawyering is much more lucrative than PI'ing, I thought as I melted into the soft upholstery.

Brent had apparently pushed the intercom, as his secretary appeared in the doorway and waited for instructions. She was a looker, dressed conservatively in a suit that showed off her best features. And she had a lot of features. I found myself staring at her and looked away. If she noticed she didn't let on. It certainly wasn't the first time she had been ogled.

"Coffee?" Brent asked.

I nodded. "Black, with a dash of sugar."

She disappeared through the door, too soon I felt. I turned my attention back to Brent who was looking at me with bemusement.

"That's Miss Jennings. Laura," he said. Then as if reading my mind he added, "yes she is quite attractive."

"Miss?" I said, my interest aroused.

"Her fiancée is an intern at Mission Hospital."

My interest flagged and I turned my attention back to the reason I was here.

"What can you tell me about the break-in that would help? Names, perhaps, or incidents that may have a bearing on the case."

Brent creased his eyebrows into a thoughtful frown. "As I told you in your office, there is nothing in my background that would be pertinent. As far as I know, I have no unhappy clients."

"You defended a few criminal cases. Were they all settled in your favor?"

"All but one," Brent said. "A pro bono case. Jack Mitchell, small time thief, served thirty days for purse snatching. The case was cut and dried. He was caught in the act and had no defense. I plea bargained the sentence. He didn't hold it against me. In fact, he seemed happy to get off so lightly."

"How long ago was that?"

"Let me see," Brent said. He flipped through the calendar on his desk. "Last April. He got out in July."

"Where is he now?"

"County jail."

"Again?"

Brent nodded. "He broke into a car in a parking lot and stole some stuff. Petty theft again, but he's a three time loser."

"Did you represent him this time?"

"No."

I grunted and mentally crossed him off the list of suspects.

"It would help," I said, "if I knew who was the target of the break-in."

Brent shifted in his chair and combed his thin mustache with his fingers.

"I gave that some thought since we talked, and I am pretty certain that William's files were the ones of interest to whoever did this. It was a hurry up job, I'm sure, and a sloppy one."

"And your files were rifled to confuse you?"

"Perhaps. But it just might be that the intruder didn't know the setup and thought that my files were William's files. Does that make sense?"

"It makes as much sense as anything else. But if what you are saying is correct, I should be investigating William's clients, or ex-clients as the case may be. It would help if we knew which file the thief was after."

Brent scratched his head. "That will be difficult. Laura would have to go through them. Unless something obvious has been altered or removed, it would be next to impossible to determine."

Laura, who had been standing in the doorway during our conversation, spoke up.

"I have a pretty good idea of what each file should contain," she said. "But it won't be easy. This could take time."

"Then let's get started," I said.

"All right. But none of the information in those files can be revealed to you, Mister Marcus."

"No need to," I said. "Miss Jennings need only tell us which files have been compromised, either because information is missing or tampered with."

Laura was not only beautiful, but efficient. By noon the following day I got a phone call from Brent.

"We found the file," he said simply.

"Tell me more," I said.

"Donaldson vs. Donaldson," Brent went on. "Julia Donaldson retained William to sue Frederick for divorce. Adultery is listed as the reason. There were pictures."

"Pictures? What kind?" I asked.

Brent chuckled. "Figure it out."

"Okay," I said. "I'm sure they were not too flattering of Frederick. So he, or someone, took them from the file."

"Evidently."

"But why? There must be copies somewhere. They could easily be replaced."

"True," Brent said. "But maybe he's counting on William's death here. A new lawyer wouldn't be aware of that."

"That's a possibility. It also throws a new wrinkle into Kenwood's murder. Frederick becomes a suspect. He had as much motive as South."

"I suppose. But that's conjecture. As is everything else we just talked about. Where do you go from here?"

"Do you have Donaldson's address?" I asked.

I heard the riffle of papers, followed by a grunt.

"1756 Miranda Drive."

"I know where it is," I said. "I think I'll pay him a call."

Miranda Drive was located in the southwest part of town, a housing development built in the late eighties, middle class, some retirees. There was nothing to recommend or condemn the area. All it told me was that Donaldson was not rich and could not afford an expensive settlement.

I wasn't too sympathetic. He should have thought of this before he started hoeing in someone else's garden.

I parked in front of 1756, killed the engine and climbed out of the car, not bothering to lock it. The flagstone walk up to the tiny porch was lined with some shrubbery, common in this area, but not one I could identify.

I pushed the doorbell and heard a faint chime. Moments later the door opened a crack and a man's face appeared.

"No soliciting," he said.

I smiled apologetically. "Mister Donaldson?" I said.

He started to shut the door, but I held my hand against it.

"I'm not a salesman. I'm a private detective."

Donaldson relaxed and the door swung open, only to stop short of allowing entrance.

"Detective?" he asked. "Is that bitch still spying on me?"

"If you are referring to your wife, the answer is no. I need to ask you a few questions."

His face betrayed interest, but he held on to the door, keeping it between him and me.

"May I come in?"

Donaldson hesitated. "Who are you working for?"

"Howard Brent."

"Never heard of him."

"He shares an office with William Kenwood."

At the mention of Kenwood, Donaldson's frown deepened.

"That bastard? I don't want to talk to anyone who is associated with him."

"You realized that Mister Kenwood is dead," I said.

"Yeah. But I'm not shedding any tears over it."

"You haven't been to his office recently?"

"I haven't been anywhere in six weeks," he said.

He opened the door wide. I stepped back as I looked at him leaning on a crutch, his right leg in a cast.

"I fell off the roof a while back. Can't get around."

"I'm terribly..." I muttered.

He cut me off. "It's probably for the best. At least I'm off the list of suspects."

"Someone tampered with your wife's file. Stole some pictures."

At the mention of pictures, Donaldson's face reddened.

"Would you have any idea who it could be?"

"Well," he said. "I wasn't the only one in those pictures. Did you ever think of that?"

As a matter of fact, I hadn't. But he was right.

"Who..." I started.

He held up a hand. "None of your business," he said.

"But it's important. A man is dead and …"

Before I could protest further, he closed the door.

———————————————

I am familiar with photographs of straying spouses. And there are only a few photographers who deal in this line of work. I use Shel Burton for my jobs. Most of the other PIs do the same. I decided to pay him a call.

Burton worked out of his home. A bachelor, he lived in a walk-up apartment not too far from my office.

It was a typical bachelor's pad: messy, with no amenities other than a wall full of pictures that he had taken over the years. Photographic equipment lay about in what appeared to be disorder. But knowing Shel as I did, I was sure he knew exactly where everything was.

When I explained the reason for my call, he shook his head.

"Yeah," he said. "I know the case you mean. Mike was the PI on that one. I got some good shots."

"Would I be breaching ethics if I asked to see them?"

He pushed aside a pile of magazines and sat down, motioning for me to do the same.

"Not at all," he said. "But I think you should know that you aren't the only one interested in those pictures."

I lifted an eyebrow. "Has someone else asked to see them?"

"No. Nobody asked. But somebody broke in here, removed them from my computer and took the CD ROM that I had them stored on." A deep frown darkened his face and he swore under his breath. "They even trashed the hard drive. They weren't taking any chances on my recovering them."

I groaned. "And you don't have hard copies?"

"I don't keep them. They take up too much space. And I can always print one out if I need it." He shook his head and added, "as a rule."

"But not in this case," I said.

"I want whoever broke in here to believe that," he said. "But just between you and me…" He grinned and held out a small plastic object that looked a little like a pill box.

"Thumb drive," he said simply. "I keep all my files on it. If anything happens to my hard drive I still have all my files."

He turned the drive over in his hand, crossed to the computer and inserted the drive into the port.

The pictures were excellent. Good quality, clear and sharp. And explicit.

I studied them with the hope of identifying the girl: young, no more than thirty, blonde, and, in the vernacular, stacked. She wore a startled expression on her face, and her hands were in the process of pulling the sheet up in a belated attempt at modesty. She only half succeeded, leaving a fully exposed breast for me to appreciate. While the pictures, under ordinary circumstances, would be entertaining, they shed no light on the identity of the lady.

I had Shel print out a set, thanked him and left.

<hr>

"So, where do you go from here?" Marge said.

I shook my head. "I have to find out who the lady is," I said. "She's the key to the whole thing. Whoever killed William Kenwood went to a lot of trouble to get rid of the pictures."

Marge stirred her coffee until I thought the spoon would dissolve, took a tentative sip, then stirred it some more. She picked up her napkin and patted her lips.

"When are you going to show me the picture?"

"I don't want you involved," I said.

She laughed. "I already am involved, luv."

"That's not what I mean."

She shrugged, pushed the coffee away from her with a grimace, and leaned back.

"Look. You need help with this. I may or may not be able to help. But we won't know unless we try. Show me the damn picture and quit being so noble. I'm not going to get hurt looking at a picture."

I studied her for a minute. She glared back at me. She was right. What harm could it do to have her look?

I reached into my pocket, took the picture out and slid it across the table. She picked it up, held it up to the light and studied it.

She smiled slightly. "Healthy girl, isn't she?" she said.

"Forget the boobs," I said. "Do you recognize her?"

"She looks familiar," she said. "She's somebody, but I can't place her at the moment. Give me some time."

I was encouraged by Marge's comment. She is a no nonsense lady, and I take her at her word. I have never been disappointed.

She held up the photo. "Can I keep this?"

I held out my hand and started to protest. But she dropped it in her purse.

"I don't think …" I started.

She snapped her purse shut and stood up. "I'll be careful. Nobody is going to see this but me." She nodded toward the tab on the table.

"Your treat?"

"Isn't it always?"

"Just thought I'd ask," she said. She gave me a peck on the cheek, and started for the door.

"Call me tonight," she said, then added, "better yet, come on over. I have an idea."

" But …" I started. She waved me to silence.

"Do you want to solve this case or don't you?"

"Of course, but …"

Another wave of the hand. "Then do as I ask. Tonight. Seven."

Before I could reply she was out of the door and across the street. Nobody moved quite as fast as Marge when she was on a mission.

I arrived at Marge's exactly at seven. I rang the doorbell. Hearing nothing from the other side of the door, I was about to ring again when it opened to reveal a striking blonde in a low-cut blouse and a miniskirt.

"Wha …" I started. Then, realizing that the blonde was in fact Marge, I stepped back and stared. "What in the hell are you doing?" I asked.

Marge primped the wig and winked. "Don't I look like your friend in the picture?" she asked. She patted her hair again.

I looked her up and down appreciatively.

"Yeah," I said. "You do at that, I suppose."

Of course I had no idea how tall the young lady in the photograph was. But facially Marge bore a remarkable resemblance to her.

Marge smoothed what there was of her skirt and smiled coyly.

"I think I should pay a visit to whatsisname."

"Who?" I asked, still studying the outfit.

"Lover boy. Donaldson."

"Look, Marge, you look a lot like our mystery woman. But you're not going to fool Donaldson. I mean, for Pete's sake, they were …"

Marge waved an impatient hand. "I know that. But I may shock him into saying something important before he realizes I'm not her. The look on his face will be worth it."

She picked up a tiny handbag that wasn't capable of holding more than a set of keys if there weren't too many of them.

"Let's go," she said.

"I …"

"What have you got to lose? Even if he doesn't fall for it, we are no worse off than we were before, are we?"

I couldn't argue with that. In fact I couldn't argue with Marge at all once she had made up her mind to do something. And if I didn't go along with this charade, she would go it alone. With a sigh to let her know I was an unwilling participant, I held the car door open for her and together we drove to Miranda Drive.

I pulled the car up to the curb in front of Donaldson's house, parking under the oak tree that bordered his property. He may remember the car, and the element of surprise would be lost if he saw me before Marge had a chance to confront him.

Marge sidled up the sidewalk, stepped to the door and pushed the button. I stood off to one side where I could hear but not be seen until Donaldson stepped outside.

The door opened just enough to allow Donaldson to peer out. Marge wiggled her fingers and smiled.

"Hi, Freddie," she said.

"Eunice? Wha …" He said. He flung the door open all the way and started outside. Then he stopped.

"Wait a minute. You're not Eunice. What the hell is going on here?"

Marge patted him on the arm. "I'm Eunice's sister, Maizie."

"She never told me she had a sister," Donaldson growled. "What the hell are you doing here?"

"Eunice is in a lot of trouble," Marge said. "Her husband found out about you two."

"Hey, I know that. We're history. I want nothing to do with her."

"He beat her, you know."

"Cary? The great Cary Burke? What a laugh."

"Eunice asked me to …" Marge started. Donaldson spotted me and his face reddened.

"You're the dick who was here the other day. What the hell is going on here?"

He glared at me, then at Marge. "Listen lady, I don't know who you are, but if you two aren't off my property in ten seconds I'm calling the cops."

Before I could reply he pulled his head back and slammed the door.

Back in the car, Marge took off the wig and threw it in the back seat.

"Cary Burke," she laughed. "The TV preacher, activist, humanitarian and keeper of our morals."

I was familiar with the name. He was a force in the state with a following in the millions. I was not one of them.

Marge was still chuckling. "Cary Burke. Freddie was beating his time with his wife. That's too funny." She laughed harder. "Do you suppose Burke is responsible for Kenwood's murder?"

I shrugged. "It would appear so. If this went public it would be quite a blow to his image."

"And his ambitions."

"What ambitions?" I asked.

"I heard he's planning to run for Governor."

"Governor? Cary Burke? That's a laugh."

"It's no laughing matter," Marge said. "He's got millions of fans and supporters."

I whistled softly. The whole scenario was beginning to make sense.

———————

"What this state needs is a man who values the things in life that count."

I watched with more than a little skepticism as Cary Burke stood at his mahogany pulpit and addressed the throng at his chapel and the viewers watching from the comfort of their homes.

"Honesty. Integrity. Morality. We cannot allow the holy institution of marriage to be sullied by allowing gays to marry. Marriage is a sacred trust between a man and a woman. Love, honor, forsake all others. My wife and I treasure those vows."

I laughed at the hypocrisy, got up and switched off the television set.

While I was certain Burke was behind the killing and the theft of Kenwood's file, I had nothing to tie him to the crimes. He was a revered public figure, the idol of the millions of decent God-fearing people who looked to him for strength and guidance. How could I possibly get anyone to believe he was a thief and a killer?

Yes, I had the photograph. But that was not enough. Burke would claim that it was a fake. With today's technology, pictures can and do lie. I could be put in the Vatican shaking hands with the Pope, and I'm a Baptist.

"Yeah," Marge agreed when I told her about this. "But there are three people who know the picture is the real deal."

"Three?" I said.

"Yeah. There's Donaldson and Eunice Burke. And there's the photographer."

"Right," I said. I had forgotten about Shel Burton.

The significance of that made me sit up straight.

"That means that Donaldson and Burton are in danger. One person is already dead. And he wasn't even involved in 'the event'." I stood up, threw a bill on the counter and started for the door.

"I've got to warn Shel," I said. "And Donaldson."

"What are you going to do after that?" Marge asked.

"Pay a visit to the Reverend."

———————

I was surprised by the relatively small size of the "Chapel of the Believers". Cary Burke's followers were legion, and I expected them all to be in attendance. But the wide-ranging power of television made it possible for them to see and hear the Reverend without getting out of bed.

I eased my way up the center aisle, found a seat a few rows from the altar and sat down. The elderly woman sitting to my left smiled at me warmly, then dropped her eyes to the program in her lap. I glanced at the program I had been handed at the door. It was the usual church curriculum consisting of prayer, hymn singing and more prayer. The sermon, the main event that everyone in attendance came to hear, would be delivered by The Reverend Cary Burke.

An usher started past me. I put out my hand and touched his sleeve. He paused, gave me a benign smile, his eyes otherwise betraying a disinterest.

I held out a manila envelope. "Would you deliver this to the Reverend for me please?"

He held up his hands. "We can't …" he started.

"This is important," I said. "Reverend Burke will be most interested in it."

The usher paused. He had heard this before, I was certain, from parishioners who wanted to have an audience with the great man and would say anything to get it.

"It concerns a photograph," I said. "If you are unwilling to deliver it, then talk to Reverend Burke. Tell them that I am in possession of a photograph. He'll know what that means."

"A photograph, Sir?" the usher said. "I don't understand."

I pushed the envelope into his hand. "This is urgent. You will be doing Reverend Burke a great favor." I smiled. "He'll thank you."

The usher looked from me to the envelope. "I don't interface with Reverend Burke. He's a very busy man, and doesn't have time for …"

"Certainly you know someone who does 'interface'. Or leave the envelope on the pulpit. The Reverend will be most interested."

There was a pause as the usher looked from me to the envelope with a puzzled frown. Seeing the resolve in my eyes, he took the envelope, holding it out from his body as if it were toxic.

"It's harmless," I said. "But nevertheless of great importance to Reverend Burke."

I nodded toward the envelope.

"Please."

He turned it over, then came to a decision. "I'll see that he gets it," he said.

"Promise me," I said. "This is most urgent."

"Promise," he said with a nod.

I relaxed. If you can't trust an usher at a religious service, who can you trust?

———••———

Cary Burke was not a big man. But what he lacked in physical stature he more than made up for in charisma. He had piercing brown eyes, a firm chin, and a rich, booming voice that gave everything he said the stamp of authority. I was mesmerized by his sermon even if I didn't believe a word of it. It wasn't difficult to see why he had such a large and dedicated following.

The services ended with a hymn I remembered from my Sunday school days, and I stood aside as the parishioners filed down the aisle and out the door. Except for a few stragglers who were holding back hoping for a glimpse or a word with Reverend Burke, the building emptied quickly. Several minutes passed after the last of them had exited when the rest of the hopefuls left as well. I was alone.

I waited. If my message had been delivered as promised I was certain that someone would come looking for me.

I wasn't disappointed. The curtain behind the altar was pushed aside by an usher I had seen earlier. He searched the room, his eyes finally settling on me. Briskly he crossed the stage and down the aisle, stopping in front of me. "Mister Marcus?"

"That's me," I said.

He bowed stiffly. "Would you come with me, please?" Without waiting for a reply he led me up to the stage and through the curtain.

Several men and women, who I assumed were staff members and aides, mingled in the small anteroom. We brushed past them to a door at the back of the room. My escort knocked softly on the door, opened it a crack and stood back. With a slight bow he swept his hand toward the door in a silent invitation.

I opened the door, took a tentative step inside, and stopped. The door shut behind me. I looked over my shoulder. My escort was not there. I was alone.

In front of me was a huge desk on which papers were stacked neatly in piles. An oversized chair sat behind it. A gooseneck desk lamp threw a soft yellow light that reflected off the polished surface. The only other furniture was a straight-backed chair facing the desk. I stood behind it and waited.

The door behind the desk opened and Reverend Burke strode through it with purposeful steps. Without speaking he motioned for me to be seated.

It was more of an order than an invitation. I sat. I was soon to learn that Burke was not one to "invite" anyone or anything.

Burke waited until I was seated, then sat down as well. He picked up a piece of paper, studied it with a frown, and then looked at me for the first time.

"Did you send this note?"

I nodded.

"What is this nonsense about a picture? I have no idea what you are talking about."

"I think you do," I said, "or else I wouldn't be sitting here."

"You are here because I received a threatening note. I don't like being threatened. I asked you here so that you can see for yourself that I am not one to trifle with. I have a reputation to uphold and a church to minister."

He leaned back, frowned at me for a minute, then leaned forward again. "Now if you have anything …"

"Yes, I do," I said. "One man is dead and at least two others are in danger because of this picture. Deny it if you will, but that won't keep it from becoming public knowledge."

He started to say something, but I held up my hand. "I have no intention of showing the photo to anyone who hasn't already seen it. But I will use it if I find it necessary. And don't get any ideas about getting rid of me. A copy of that photo is safely tucked away, but if anything should happen to me I have left instructions to go public with it."

"Do you realize who you are dealing with?" he asked.

"Yeah," I replied. "I'm dealing with a man who has a big PR problem if a certain picture was to become public."

Silence. I watched as Burke's stern frown dissolved into a melancholy expression. He tapped his fingers on the polished desktop, leaned forward and looked me in the eye.

"How much?" he said.

I gave what I hoped was a derisive laugh. "Do I look like a blackmailer?"

"I don't know what a blackmailer looks like," he said. "But I can't think of another reason for your being here."

"I was hired to find out who broke into my client's office and stole documents from his file. I will be reporting back to him when I leave here. While I have no proof, I am convinced that you, or more correctly, one of your men, did so."

"And why would I do such a thing?"

"The picture, of course. If there was ever any doubt, the break-in at the photographer's office is proof enough. And Kenwood's murder."

Burke nodded, but said nothing.

"If you insist on denying it, the picture will be Exhibit A. Who else would be interested in keeping it from becoming public?"

Burke shifted in his chair. "Exactly what do you want from me?"

"That's for my client to decide," I said. "I am here to let you know that you are the number one suspect, and anything you may say or do will only make matters worse for you."

"I see," he said. "How kind of you."

"Sarcasm aside," I said, "you may want to reconsider your political ambitions. If you don't, I guarantee you the infamous photo will surface. Politics and politicians are ruthless, and no matter how hard you try to hide your skeletons, someone will find them."

"I will take that under advisement," he said.

"I was hired to look into the break-in. I am satisfied that I have found my man."

Burke shrugged his shoulders dismissively, his face expressionless.

"Kenwood's murder, however, is the real crime. So you can bet my report will be of interest to the authorities. I don't know what your opinion is of the police, but don't sell them short. They are very good at putting two and two together." I leaned back and folded my hands across my chest. "It's your call."

A vein stuck out in Burke's temple and he glared at me from across the desk.

"Listen, Mister … er …" he glanced at the envelope. " Mister Marcus. I have connections, important connections in this town. I can't be bullied."

"I'm sure you do, Reverend," I said. "And if you think they can prevent embarrassing pictures from seeing the light of day, then go for it."

Burke sighed and stood up. He picked up a ledger from the desk and opened it.

"Every man has a price," he said, pulling a pen from his pocket. "Name yours."

I laughed. "Come now, Reverend. Certain things in this life are not for sale. My integrity is one of them." I stood up and started for the door. Putting my hand on the doorknob, I turned back to Burke.

"You know what has to be done if you don't want a scandal."

Burke ignored my remark. "Eunice is a saint. And I will do anything to protect her good name," he went on. "This is all a misunderstanding. A man in my position is a target of those who wish to see my good works …."

"Spare me the sermon, Reverend," I said.

I left him talking to himself.

"He called her 'a saint'?" Marge laughed. "There's another word that starts with 's' and ends in 't' that is more descriptive."

"Eunice may be an adulteress, but that doesn't make her a bad person."

"The last time I checked, it wasn't a requirement for sainthood, either."

"Whatever," I said. "Eunice Burke isn't the issue."

I picked up the newspaper from the table and pointed to an article buried on page three: "Lawyer's Slayer Turns Himself In."

"Don't you think it's significant that this guy appears from out of the blue and confesses to killing Kenwood?" I said. "He claimed it was an accident. He'll probably get off with a year or two."

"Yeah," Marge agreed. "And a bundle of cash from our friend Burke."

"It's an investment," I said. "No trial, no embarrassing evidence. He's heading 'em off at the pass."

She took a tentative sip of coffee, made her usual face and reached for the sugar.

"Smart move," she said. "You must have shaken him up. Have you heard the latest about Burke?"

I shook my head.

"Burke issued a statement this morning. He is withdrawing from the gubernatorial race. It would 'interfere with my ministering to my flock,' Ain't that a hoot?" She put her head back and laughed.

"Not to mention a certain photograph," I said.

"Ah, yes," Marge said. "Still, it's a pretty good shot of old Eunice. It shows her best side. Pity to waste it."

I laughed. "Marge, you are incorrigible."

I reached for the bill, but Marge snatched it from my hand.

"This one's on me. For a job well done. Now I guess it's back to straying spouses."

The thought was sobering. But, as I said, it's a living.

Our next story takes a decidedly sharp turn toward the dark side. A young man in search of company on a summer night finds more than he had bargained for in L.E. Schwaller's "Everybody Knows This Is Nowhere".

Mr. Schwaller's work has received numerous awards, including a first prize from Rambunctious Review for his story, "Flood", and the Carol Muske-Dukes Award for "The Exorcism of Diablo-Muerte in 1973". His poetry and creative non-fiction may be found in Infectus and other literary journals.

Everybody Knows This Is Nowhere

by L.E. Schwaller

"Say something," there was a pause filled with solemnity, then a whimper. "Anything. Please, say anything."

But no words came to mind, and in silence I stared at the watery void of the Moreau River below where we had just tossed a body. The drop from the bridge to the black water was a good forty feet, and yet I could see the ripples, the wake, ebbing against the mud and brush bramble shoreline until the waters stilled and became one with the current that continued peacefully downstream.

I was sweating, sticky with gnats, and a fat mosquito nipped at my neck. My throat was raw, my mouth drying from the fading drunk and the struggle of crudely enshrouding a heavy body in tacky bedding and then weighing it down with chain and rocks before dragging it all to the precipice to heave it over the edge. I shook my head, still searching for words of impossible comfort, then stared down again at the river to seek out the secrets it kept somewhere in that darkness.

Not six hours before, I had been sipping warming Budweiser, the rural breeze sweeping across the porch of my parents' country house. My father was out there with me, leaning back in his tattered lawn chair as he stared blankly out at the nothingness. I would take a swig and watch him as he belched then stroked his swollen gut before letting off a dialectal of meaningless grunts.

This was the extent of what we had to say to one another, and I can't say I wanted it any other way. Mother was still in the kitchen cleaning up after dinner, scrubbing at a pan encrusted with burnt pot roast, the light above the sink inviting in moths and June bugs through the torn screen door. This was the same scene that had sent me off—off to the Navy, college, Chicago. Their faces and this house had chronicled the harsh years since I had left. He was more bloated now, his body finally beginning to show signs of breaking down with the wear and tear of his habits. She was a gaunt shell of the woman I had known, having spent her life hunched over the stove or the dishes or any other archaic expectation of a woman in that place.

It was the homecoming I had expected in a way, and within ten minutes of trying to tolerate the banality of the summer night I knew so well—the country blackness that has nothing better to do than listen to itself chirp and whine and bray—I asked myself why the hell I had come back and then took the car and a handful of beers and made the long drive into town.

When I reached Nick's Bar, it was a quarter to nine. The happy hour crowd had gone home to their children and spouses, and the late-night karaoke twenty-somethings would leave the rest of us in peace for another hour or so. Part of me had hoped to see a friend, a familiar face, but it had been years since I had so much as spoken to anyone from back home. I had expected swinging honky-tonk and meth, bad tattoos and Marlboro Reds. However, that wasn't the case. No, instead I found myself disappointed to be in a bar like any other, drunk and staring forward at nothing in particular while the jukebox filled the room with sad country music.

I didn't seek her out, no, but I didn't shy away either. We shared coy glances across the L-shaped bar and clichéd winks and nods back and forth. Finally she took the stool next to me and bought us each a boilermaker. We sat close to one another and she leaned forward so I could see down her blouse. She ordered us a round of shots, then another, and within an hour we were in her car, drunkenly fingering and groping at each other as she sped down State Route C away from town and toward the dark, wild country hills of the northern Ozarks.

As she made the turn onto her gravel drive, I kissed her neck. She smelled of sweat and perfume and moaned as I tongued and nibbled on her ear. I was jolted away from her by a rut in the road and sat back as we approached her prefab home that had been installed on a lawn of crabgrass at the edge of a rolling and wild field. The house was all yellow siding and lawn ornaments, the plastic and overgrowth meshing so they could decay together. In a generation it would dilapidate, much in the way my childhood home had, and given another or two it would be gone, swallowed up by time, the gravel road washing away and being retaken by the hay grasses and brush from which it had been carved in the naïve hopes of a better life and future.

Hunting dogs pent off to the side of the house barked, and in the singing porch light, her smile-lines and the heavy, dark bags beneath her eyes shone with an unflattering clarity. So I pulled her close to me for a kiss and then took her inside. Her body was swollen, plump, and we went at each other with a drunken fervor and lust that pulled us together at our basest and most primal parts. We locked as one, an alligator wrestling match that went grinding and tonguing its way across the Berber carpet of the living room and down the hall where I tore off her blouse and pants. She had sour whiskey and smoke on her breath and loved me with every inch of her (and there were many inches). In turn, I gave her the attention she deserved, needed, kissing and prodding all the real estate I could. And it was when things got heated, truly heated, that the dogs erupted again, barking.

We stopped our motion and listened to him—her husband—as he crashed through the front door. The two of us remained still, our arms wrapped around one another. I could feel myself retreating from her, shrinking, as I heard his labored march down the hall, drunkenly bouncing from one wall to the other.

She pushed me upwards, commanding me: "Get in the closet!"

I scrambled off of her and stole into the closet quickly and without pants. Once inside, I peered through the slats in the door and watched as her husband fell into the bedroom. He was in that special place beyond mere drunkenness and stumbled about with a bottle of bourbon in one hand and that goddamn revolver in the other.

"Where is that son-of-a-bitch?" Her husband slurred as he jammed his shin into the corner of the cheap water bed and fell forward before righting himself with his crutches: the gun barrel and the bottle.

"There ain't nobody here," she said, smiling up at him, her body scarcely covered by the twisted sheets. "Come to bed."

"The hell there ain't," he spoke with a drawl, that twang that made me hate him. "I know you got someone here with you."

"Who's here? What in God's name are you hollerin' about?"

"I can smell it on you," he bent down and sniffed at the sheets. "I can smell him on our bed."

"Put that goddamn gun away," she scolded him as he stumbled over my boots and nearly fell to the floor.

I squinted, looking out through the slats of the closet door. Her husband was a thin man, a gangly, bowlegged cowboy with an angular face. His jeans were caked with dried splatters of cement and dusted white and his eyes were tired.

"You're drunk, Sam."

"You're drunk, you goddamn whore."

A silence followed his rebuttal and then another stumble. The smell was there, on my body. Her smell. And in that moment I prayed, truly and hypocritically prayed he wouldn't sniff me out, my naked, stinking person hiding in the blue black light of his closet.

But the man, Sam, had forgotten all about his keen sense of smell and decided instead to go on interrogating her. He accused her of infidelities, listing off all the men she had supposedly brought home to their marital bed as he called her a whore again and again. She pulled her knees to her chest and righted herself against the headboard, replying with dry wit and unflinching sass to his jabs and barbs. And it was then, as he went on and on, parading about the room while she mocked and cut him at every turn, that it all seemed almost a show, a kind of play with lines they'd rehearsed and then delivered ad nauseam until it all grew stale and tired.

"He in there?" Sam, her husband, pointed to the closet—to me, to my nakedness—with the barrel of his gun, then returned it back to his hip.

"You don't know what you're talking about." The playfulness had left her and she pleaded with him: "Just stop it."

"Is he hiding in my closet?"

I was focused on the revolver; the butt, the chambers, the hammer, the long nose, the angle of the barrel, watching it rise again, slowly, slowly from the floor. His eyes followed, dreary and clouded, working to focus on the gun, the sights, the door. Sam was looking at me in that moment; I knew it, looking at me through the slats, looking me in the eyes. He was going to aim. I felt my body tense, every hair on end, pricking and panicking.

"Stop it, just stop it," she screamed. "You're scaring me."

He turned to her: "What the hell have you got to …"

I burst from my sanctuary, throwing open the cheap closet door with such force that it splintered to bits against the wall. I never took my eyes off of his arm or the gun. He stumbled backwards as I threw the heft of my naked weight into him. But he didn't lose his footing. I grappled at the gun, clenching into his wrist with my fingernails. He stomped on my bare foot with the heel of his boot and the pain exploded up my leg like a shot. I elbowed him in the bridge of his nose. But neither of us would release our hold on the share we had claimed of the revolver.

"Kill him," I heard her holler over the commotion. "Just kill him, for Christ's sake. I'm bored of this."

It was then that the gun involuntarily fired, the thunderous pop filling the room. He and I kept after one another, fighting for our claim to the pistol until I lost my grip and, with little else to do, clenched my fist, aimed for the pointed tip of his nose, and punched him in the face. He faltered this time and fell backwards, dropping the gun to the carpet where it fired once more.

We were winded, heaving and choking for breath as we huffed in the acrid, sulfurous gun smoke that settled on the bedroom.

"You're naked," he said, thoughtlessly.

"Sorry," I replied.

"She's dead."

I looked up and saw it was true. She was still seated, her back against the headboard, but her knees had fallen to the side and the sheet was no longer covering her. Her right breast was exposed and I could see the candy-red divot glistening in the yellow moonlight that split through the drab, beaten curtains.

"You shot her."

"I didn't shoot nothing," he said. "I never aimed the gun."

"What in Christ's name are you talking about?"

"I barely keep it loaded," he said, examining the pistol.

I held my hands to the ceiling and thought he might shoot me dead where I stood, but he never bothered to look up. Instead he tossed the gun to the side and picked himself up off the floor.

"It's a game we play," he said, looking down at his dead wife. "She never actually has nobody with her …"

"I'm sorry," I said again as I cupped my nakedness and searched the room for my pants. "But intention or not, that's your gun and your game."

"But I didn't aim it!"

"I don't care. Neither did I!"

"Oh yes you did. Struggling with me for it. You pointed it right at her."

"What are you saying?"

"I'm saying you killed her."

"Bullshit," I said, still short of breath.

"Yes, you surely did. You aimed it, I fired," he said, his brow furrowed. "You're my accomplice. We're a team."

I tried to argue, to reason with him. But there was no use, so I just shook my head.

"We're a team," he repeated with a nod. "And like it or not, we either figure this out or we burn together."

His broken logic, the beer, the backwoods breeze rustling the curtains, I heard it all, whispering to me. I couldn't help myself. The bullet was in her chest and the mortal wound stared at us, a rubicund eye above her naked breast. What choice did I have? Could we call the sheriff? Explain ourselves? There would be questioning, background checks. Maybe even a trial. I'd never get out of the state.

"What do we do?"

"We gotta get rid of her," he said, calculation stirring somewhere in that drunkenness. He took a step back to examine the moment and weighed her with his eyes.

"How are we supposed to do that?" I was pulling on one of my boots as I hopped about the room, my pants still unbuttoned, belt jangling.

"We could chop her up?"

"That's your wife, man," I said. "And with what?"

"Hell, I don't know," he threw up his arms. "I'm just spitballin' here."

I watched as he approached the bed and took two fistfuls of the sheets and began yanking at her heft until her body fell to the floor with a dead, heavy thud. He then tugged and tucked at the bedding to envelop her in a cocoon of tired blankets and moist sheets before squatting down and shaking out his shoulders as he prepared to leverage his weight against hers. With a grunt, he wrenched at her ankles, pulling as hard as he could until she slipped from his fingers and he fell over backwards. He laughed as his feet went above his head and kicked a corner lamp, the awkward violence of which split the tacky gold lamp stand in two and shattered the bulb against the wall.

"Are you just going to stand there watching?" He grinned up at me from the floor, the dim light slicing between the curtains to sketch his pointed chin, those gaunt, bony cheeks, and the dead space where a bottom tooth had once been. Then he laughed again.

I slipped my t-shirt over my head, sobered by the moment and circumstance, and crossed the room to help. We clenched the sheets and blankets as we carted her with short, waddling steps down the dim hallway. He kicked open the front screen door and we shuffled across the concrete slab they called a porch and out into the light of the drive, he backwards and looking over his shoulder, I awkwardly grappling about her as I did the best I could to keep my grip.

"It'd be easier to carry her if we cut her up."

"I know," I said, struggling and pinching at the blankets, praying they wouldn't open and let her fall out onto the pale white gravel. "But again, how do you suggest we do that?"

"Hell," he groaned and let her fall. The bedding was jerked from my fingers and her head whipped as it thumped against the rocky front drive, and I cursed.

"Just shut up, will you?"

"I'm just saying," he went on. "We could make this all a hell of lot easier by cutting her up."

"Do you know how hard it is to cut a person up?"

"I've seen them in movies doing it with samurai swords."

"Do you have a samurai sword?"

"Well, no, but we got an ax and a chainsaw. I filled it up with gas just the other day and the teeth was sharpened this past spring."

"That's your wife, man!"

He nodded and gave a shrug before bending down to claw at her ankles to find his grip. I followed in turn, wriggling my fingers beneath her soft shoulders and locking them on the underside of her. Then we began our waddling dance once more, continuing on until we bridged the back-breaking distance to the bed of his Chevy where we managed to shove the mass of blankets and sheets and spouse.

"What the hell are we going to do with her? And if you say chop her up one more goddamn time I'm going to punch you in the mouth."

Sam snorted and then, after what felt like eons of thought, suggested we weigh down the body and sink her. I agreed for lack of better ideas, and so we set about the task of rooting around the drive and yard for rocks and stones. Sam was hurried, scurrying like a horny beagle as he stumbled back and forth. We gathered a pile of rocks and broken bits of cinder block and gravel and built them into a sort of cairn in the driveway behind Sam's truck. Once we had amassed what he deemed to be enough, Sam climbed into the bed of the Chevy and unwrapped the shroud of blankets. She was on her back, naked and staring up at the sky with open, motionless eyes. We both turned away in silence then began to pack the rocks in around her.

At first I was compelled to place them gently between her limbs and around her head. But Sam wasn't inclined to be slowed by reverence and instead worked quickly, tossing the stones and chips of block on her and tucking the dirt-covered rocks into unspeakable places. Once we had run out of the bigger stuff, we each took up fistfuls of chalky gravel and poured them overtop her. Then Sam told me to wait a bit and ran off across the drive toward the tin shed where he disappeared into the dark and crashed about. As he dug, audibly, through tools and storage, I wrapped and covered her up again with the sheets and blankets, taking care to tie the ends together so nothing could slip out.

Within a few minutes, Sam emerged from the shed with a length of heavy chain clanking as it dragged behind him. I held up one of her ends so Sam could slip the chain beneath her before bringing it up and around again. He repeated this over and over, wrapping her tightly from head to toe in chain before securing it with a heavy lock so she couldn't come loose and float to the top of the water where people might discover her. Then we closed up the bed of the truck and set off to dump her in the river somewhere.

Against my better judgment, I let Sam drive since it was his truck. He eased us down the gravel drive and out onto the blacktop fine, but after a mile or two he got restless and started to paw under the bench seat as he drove.

"Will you keep your eyes on the goddamn road," I said as I reached over him and took hold of the wheel to keep us from drifting off the winding highway.

He came up with a bottle of Old Crow and retook the wheel then spun off the lid with a stroke of his thumb. It seemed he was sobering up quick and had decided it better to keep drinking. After taking two large swigs, he pushed the bottle toward me. I took a pull and sensed the burn roll down my throat and chest and into my stomach where it warmed me from the inside out. I felt my face flush and cranked down the window to let the night air fill the stale cab of the truck.

The blacktop rolled up and down and around through the dark country. Sam leaned on the gear shifter and held tight, focused, as we swayed into the turns. He put the pedal all the way down and the old truck roared down the straightaways. I watched him as we passed beneath the street lamps at the end of a family drive. With a stuttering glimpse, I could see him flare his dry, red nose and lick at his curled lips. He breathed heavy but held a deliberate, pierced glare through the wash of drunkenness.

We shared another drink after he took a turn onto Old Loesch Road. The gravel was loose and pounded against the underside of the pickup like hail on a metal roof, and the truck sent up a cloud of dust behind us that blotted out all we had left. Ahead, the road was lit white in the high beams. It crowned in the middle and fell off steep on either side, with deep troughs lining the path. I remembered this drive. We were headed toward the bridge that ran overtop the Moreau River, which was just downstream from a swimming hole I had frequented as a boy.

In the summers, my childhood friends and I had spent hours upon end in those muddied waters, swinging off a rope tied to a towering tree that leaned above the calm pool some hundred yards upriver from the bridge. We'd wear shoes as to not cut our feet on the sharp rocks or the broken glass that ended up in the swimming hole when people had too much to drink. My uncle had shown us boys where we could jump off the bridge without getting hurt on the slick boulders that hid just below the surface of the water. He was drunk and cautioned that you had to jump in that one spot and only that spot or you would break your legs on the rocks. He demonstrated by standing on the concrete ledge of the bridge, poised like a high diver above the water in a pair of dripping cutoff jeans that he had made into swim trunks with a pocketknife. We leaned over the edge and watched him bound off backwards, twisting through the air and splashing into the water with a deafening smack. When he came up he gave a hoot, and I shoved my way in front of my friends to make sure I got to jump next.

It was when I was a teenager that a boy got killed and they stopped letting people swim there. Signs were posted all over and people ignored them for a while, but then they ironed up the drive with a locked gate, and over time the love for the place was overcome by the ten minute walk through the itchweed that it took to get down to the gravel bar where everyone sat their coolers and lawn chairs and beach towels for that time between dips. I hadn't known the boy who died, but he had gone to my old grade school. He hit his head when he tried to do a cannonball off the bridge, and they said he went under and never came up. Not so much as a bubble. The water of the Moreau rolls real slow, but at first they couldn't find his body despite hours of searching. In fact, it took a good week, if I remember right. There was a storm with flash flooding some days after he went under, and then someone discovered his broken body tangled up in a root mess of a downed tree in the Scrivner Road wildlife preserve.

This old abandoned swimming hole was the perfect place for what Sam and I had to do. We bent around with the road and the scene opened forth a shadowy mass of trees swaying on the hot breeze. Sam ground the truck to a halt in the middle of the bridge and booted open his door before stumbling out and working his way to the back of the pickup. I followed suit, feeling tight from the whiskey.

He pulled up on the rusted tailgate, yanked it loose, and I winced at the deafening echo that folded out onto the open river bottom. And then I realized we were alone, utterly alone, and I wasn't sure what he had done with the revolver.

"Are you going to toss the gun in, too?" I asked and strained to recall whether or not he had picked it up off the bedroom floor.

"Back at the house where we left it," he said.

I eyed him carefully, but he remained seemingly unconcerned with anything save the task at hand, standing at the bed of the truck and shaking his head at the hulking mass of chain and bedding. I asked him if he thought he had the strength to get her over the ledge and into the water.

"There ain't nothin to it," he said before reaching forward into the bed and pulling at the chains to inch her backwards.

I looked across the bridge and up the road that led away from the river bottom and snaked into the trees and hills, expecting headlights to come streaming down and around the bend at any moment, but there was nothing. Turning in the direction from which we had come, I saw there was only darkness still, the dust trail we had left on the road having all but settled. In the distance, out over the fields of petite stalks of growing sweet corn, the lightless tree line shimmied on the death rattle of a gust and then was tranquil once more. I stood there for a moment and listened again to the summer nights of my youth.

Sam cursed and I turned back to help him, reaching into the bed to get hold of her, and then we tugged in waves. We were getting tired and the drunk was starting to wear off again. The two of us grappled and pulled, grunting as we dragged her, inch by inch. I was beginning to sweat, my shirt bunching up in my armpits. We took turns blaming the other for not putting in his fair share. Then, with a final heave, she fell out of the truck and onto the ground with a bulky clunk.

"What are you going to do about the house?" I asked, wheezing as I gazed down at the heavy mess. "The bullet hole?"

"Don't worry about that," he said in one long, exhausted breath. "That gun ain't registered and I'm thinking I might burn the house down."

"You're going to torch your own house?"

"Makes the most sense at this point considering ain't nobody going to find her if we done this right. Everyone knows we fight all hours and they wouldn't be surprised to hear she up and left," he paused. "And to tell the truth, I never much liked that house and it's insured well enough. Maybe I'll say we got in fight and she said she was going to leave, then I came home to it all burnt up. Don't you worry none about that anyway. All that matters is we get her under the water where she can't be found and before anybody comes along this road."

"That may actually work," I said. "Burning the house down, I mean."

"Don't see why not," he said.

"But what about me?"

"What about you?"

"How do I fit into all of this?"

"Hell, son, I don't even know your name," Sam gave a kind of tired laugh. "You don't have to fit anywhere."

In that moment, when his backwardness was at its most lucid, he squatted down to ready himself for the final dead lift and I caught sight of his belt. The gun was nowhere to be seen and he was good to his word. It was back at the house just as he had said, and I had no reason not to trust him. Sam was a strange man, bred of that awkward country I had once known so well, to be sure, but he was honest. I had somehow all but forgotten that code of ethics, that misguided, almost ignorant sense of honor and fairness that sometimes gets muddled and obscured by the illiteracy and racist colloquialisms of my home. I could have killed him at any time and dumped him in that water along with his wife. But under the circumstances, what would've been the point? This entire nightmare was nearly over, and I found as we stood in the stifling Missouri air that I had begun to actually like him.

"Now grab her feet there," he said, pointing toward the other end of her.

"I thought this was her head?"

"It don't matter," he said. "Just help me get her up on the edge and we'll shove her over."

We counted off to three and then lifted in unison. The chains cut into my hands as I clenched tightly and pulled upwards. I felt as if my back would break. She might have been a thousand pounds and the sweat was pouring down my forehead, running into my eyes and stinging. Neither of us wavered or weakened, though, as we brought her up and shifted her onto the concrete ledge of the bridge. Then, with one more count, we put our weight into her and she toppled over the edge and into the blackness of the Moreau River.

I nearly went over with her, carried by my own momentum. I leaned over the side and saw the oblong mass splash into the water. Ripples the color of ink cast off in all directions and she was gone.

Sam muttered something inaudible as I stepped away from the ledge. He was looking downward still, staring at the water some forty feet below. I watched on as he shook his head and forced his eyes shut.

"You all right?" I was beginning to worry that he had sobered all the way up and would ruin the whole thing.

"We can't leave it like this," he said. "We can't walk away like we done nothing and she ain't gone."

"I'm sorry, Sam, but someone might come along." I spoke slowly and with an air of sympathy as I put my hand on his shoulder.

"We got to say something," he said, choking up as the finality, the gravity of it all seemed to lodge itself deep in his chest. "Something's got to be said, and I don't think I can bring myself to do it."

There was a long and uncomfortable silence.

"Anything," he repeated as he fought back tears. "Please, say anything."

I turned to the water again. Gnats buzzed in my ear and I swatted at a mosquito that bit the back of my neck. Finally, I squared my shoulders to the river, resting one hand on top of the other and placing them in front of my waist like a preacher.

"Mona was a good woman," I started.

"Deborah," he interrupted.

"Huh?"

"Her name was Debbie."

"Oh," and I apologized once more.

Return with us now to those golden years of detective stories, where the idle rich throw sumptuous parties on ships and murderers are found out by observation and deduction.

Percy Spurlark Parker has been publishing mysteries for over forty years and has been an active member of Mystery Writers of America and The Private Eye writers of America for just about as long.

A costume party on a ferryboat, what could go wrong? This is Mr. Parker's second story featuring the Mistress of Detection. Let us hope there are more to come.

The Ferry Tail Murder

by Percy Spurlark Parker

The Dragon Tail ferry was one of two ferryboats that bisected the Mississippi three times a day, connecting the township of Sunny Ridge with the village of Oliver Heights. Once a year Millicent Hopewell, one of Oliver Heights' most prominent citizens, chartered the Dragon Tail, since it was the larger of the two boats, for her masquerade charity ball.

This years' theme was fairy tale characters, of which she had anointed herself as queen, evident by her pale blue ball gown and diamond tiara. Just which queen of which fairy tale no one had yet to ask. Of the two hundred and thirty-seven guests, Millicent personally counted eleven Snow Whites, eighteen Red Riding Hoods, and twenty-six Cinderellas.

But when the only Rapunzel, emerging designer Abby Growith, was found in a storage room strangled by her six-foot long wig, Millicent turned to one of the seven pairs of Hansel and Gretel, to W.W. Willowby, known for her true crime novels as the Mistress of Detection.

W.W. stood at the door examining the small storage room. The body of Abby Growith was at an awkward angle on the floor in the far corner.

The room, no more than six by eight feet, W.W. judged, was dominated by shelves of cleaning supplies, and racks for brooms and mops, although now a number of brooms and mops were on the floor as well.

Abby Growith had put up a struggle, W.W. surmised. She was sprawled among the brooms and mops that had been dislodged from their rack. The smell of chlorine permeated the air from a spilled bottle of bleach that had been knocked off a lower shelf, along with an assortment of rags and spray cans.

W.W. carefully entered the room, knelt by the body and tried to find a pulse. Failing to do so, she stood, and not wanting to contaminate the crime scene any further, she made her exit, making certain to step around the spilled bleach on the floor.

Her husband stood just outside the storeroom, tall and fit, his frameless glasses not obscuring his clean-shaven face. Millicent Hopewell was there also, along with the ferry's captain, and a member of the boat's crew.

W.W. and Roy were in Raggedy Ann and Andy costumes. Being invited to the ball late, the nursery rhyme costumes were the only ones left in their sizes.

"Don't worry, babe. No one will know the difference," Roy had said, and as usual he was correct. They were more than just husband and wife. They were a writing team. Roy had done the research for every novel she'd ever written, and she constantly praised his thoroughness.

"Has anyone notified the police?" W.W. asked.

"I did," the captain said, behind his thick gray beard. "They'll be waiting back at Oliver Heights when we dock."

"This is simply awful," Millicent said. "Who could have done such a thing?"

"Random acts of violence occur every day," W.W. replied. "But we're too confined here to suggest this was random." How the body had gotten to the storage room wasn't a great mystery. Two scenarios easily presented themselves. The victim was obliviously waylaid on her way to the washroom that was just down the corridor, or had a pre-arranged meeting set, not suspecting it would be her last.

"The odds are very much in favor that the crime was committed by someone who knew her," W.W. continued. "Family or friend. Now strangulation is typically a male method of murder, but we shouldn't exclude the women in her life. Do you have a guest list, Mrs. Hopewell?"

"Yes. There's one in the captain's stateroom."

"Good, I'll need to take a look at it. Captain, if could post someone at the storage room door."

"Of course."

W.W. and Roy had learned of the charity ball when they stopped in Oliver Heights for a short visit with Edith Lagner, the editor of the Oliver Heights Review. W.W. and Edith first met when they were journalism students at NYU, resulting in a friendship that had lasted for the past thirty years. W.W. had looked forward to the ball as a pleasant interlude between the rigors of promoting her latest book, which took an in depth look at executions through the ages. But, at last, she was faced with another murder that begged to be solved.

Edith interrupted them, as they were about to enter the captain's stateroom. She and W.W. were refilling their punch glasses when W.W. was called away.

"Well, is there a big mystery afoot?" she asked, her delicately thin eyebrows rising. "Has someone absconded with the Queen's jewels?" She was one of the Snow Whites, and her curly black wig and lightly powered make-up took years off her already youthful appearance. It was one of the things W.W. envied about her; she looked as vibrant now as she had on graduation day.

"I'm afraid it's more serious than a theft," W.W. said.

There had been a hint of gayety in Edith's tone, laughter in her expression. But she sobered somewhat. "What do you mean?"

"There's been a murder, Edith. I must ask you to keep this to yourself. We don't want to alarm the rest of the passengers."

"Of course," she said, but then the newspaperwoman in her came out, "as long as I get an exclusive?"

"I don't see that as being a problem."

A wink from Edith sealed their agreement.

Checking the guests list produced the victim's fiancé, Jeff Batoni, her business partner, Karen Dartley, and her sister and brother-in-law, Rose and Nathan Hamilton.

The captain's stateroom wouldn't accommodate all of them, so W.W. requested they gather in the crew's mess hall, an oblong room with six wooden chairs on both sides of a sturdy looking metal table.

Befittingly, Abby's fiancé was dressed as Rumpelstiltskin. When he removed his twisted-nose mask, W.W. found him to be quite handsome, sandy brown hair, deep set blue eyes, a somewhat rugged, outdoorsman's square chin.

W.W. sat directly across the table from him, Abby's sister and brother-in-law were next to him on his left, and Abby's business partner a chair further down. Roy sat next to W.W. on their side of the table, Millicent next to him. The ferryboat's captain and two crew members stood by the door. One of which looked very formidable, with rolled up sleeves and hairless, tattooed forearms.

"Is someone going to tell me what this is all about?" the fiancé asked.

"I guess that falls on my shoulders, Mr. Batoni," W.W. said, referring to the guest list. She hated this part of any investigation. "I regret to inform you that Ms. Growith is dead. Her body was found just a short time ago."

Her announcement got a variety of reactions from the other side of the table. Shock expressed in gasps and wild-eyed stares erupted in the small mess hall.

"What do you mean, dead?" Jeff Batoni asked.

"That can't be," Rose said, wrinkles growing on her forehead.

"Who the hell are you to say something like this?" Nathan wanted to know.

"Stop this nonsense. I want to see Abby right now," Jeff said.

"Alright, alright," the captain's voice boomed out, reverberating off the walls as he took a step forward. "Let's have some control here. I don't like this one bit myself, but the fact is a young lady has been murdered, and we're not going to get anywhere by yelling at each other."

"Murdered," the word was almost muttered in unison by those hearing the news.

Abby's sister leaned forward, tears swelling up in her eyes. "Millicent, is this true? Please, tell me you're joking."

"We're not joking, Rose," Millicent said, shaking her head. "Someone killed poor Abby. I wish it wasn't so, but I've seen the body. That's why I've asked Mrs. Willowby to help us if she can. She's a world renowned criminologist."

"So, what is this, some kind of inquisition?" Nathan asked. "You don't suspect one of us, do you?"

"On the contrary," W.W. said. "Consider this part of the preliminary investigation. Someone on this boat has committed murder. There are over two hundred names on this guest list. With your help, perhaps we'll be able to weed out some of those listed. Give the police a better chance at pinpointing the murderer."

Nathan nodded, seemingly accepting her explanation even though she wasn't being completely truthful. She felt sure the murderer was one of those sitting across the table from her.

Rose and Nathan Hamilton's chosen costumes for the ball were Cinderella and Prince Charming. Entering the mess hall, Rose's white ruffle laden gown brushed against the sides of the narrow doorway, and she'd had some trouble sitting on the narrow wooden chair. As for Nathan, befitting his princely costume, he was dashing in a royal blue tunic with thick gold piping. The only drawback being a few minor white smudges on the toe of one of his knee high leather boots.

"I still want to see her for myself," Jeff said.

"I understand, Mr. Batoni. But I'm sorry, we simply can't allow anyone else to view the body just yet," W.W. added.

Jeff slumped backed in his chair, shoulders sagging. "This is all just too unreal."

"Do either of you know if Ms. Growith has been having problems with anyone lately?" W.W. asked to the group as a whole.

They all shook their heads, no.

"I …" Millicent started, stopped a moment as she bit her bottom lip. "Forgive me, Jeff. I don't mean to point fingers, but I did see you and Abby arguing earlier tonight."

Jeff shot her with what best could be described as a dagger stare, eye narrowing tightly. But he quickly composed himself. "A spat, nothing more. It was routine with Abby. As much as I loved her, Abby wasn't always the easiest person to live with. This time I'd gotten us here a little late and she couldn't let it go."

"My sister was a very headstrong woman," Rose said, in Jeff's defense. The long dangling curls of her costume wig played peek-a-boo with her diamond earrings. "Arguments were a part of her make-up. My husband can attest to that."

"It's true," Nathan said. "We used to be partners, but I couldn't handle her constant bickering. I was glad when Karen came along and bought me out six months ago. She's been getting the brunt of Abby's rages lately."

Karen Dartley shrugged at the end of the table. She was one of the Red Riding Hoods, her cape resting crookedly on her shoulders. "Sure we fought," she said, brushing back a lock of auburn hair from her forehead. "Hot and heavy, but all verbally, that is. We never came close to lifting a hand to each other. The arguments just kind of got the best out of both of us. Got the motivational wheels going. We'd bounce a lot of ideas off of each other. She'd never admit it, but I could see your influence in her work, Nathan. You were good for her when you were together."

"Thanks for the nod," Nathan said. "Too often people forget where they got their inspiration from."

"I'm only telling the truth," Karen said. "That's the way it was with Abby. The arguments were an intricate part of who she was. We worked hard. We argued loudly. One thing embellished the other. It got her creative juices flowing."

"Abby was a bit of a hot head," Millicent admitted meekly.

"A talented hot head," Karen added. "She could take a central theme, a thread of an idea and do wonders with it. Make it entirely her own. I said I used to throw ideas at her, but she was really the artist, my expertise has always been more on the business end. We'd just signed a contract with a major clothing chain. So, for me, dealing with Abby's violate nature was worth it." She paused. "Certainly you of all people, Mrs. Willowby, should be able to understand the drive behind Abby's argumentative ways. The creative force it released."

W.W. nodded. "There is some merit in what you say," she said, thinking of times when she and Roy budded heads over central ideas.

"Great," Jeff barked loudly. "My fiancé is dead and everyone is patting each other on the back. Isn't someone going to try to find out who killed her?"

"I believe I already have the answer to that," W.W. said.

She'd actually had a suspect in mind as they came into the dinning area. By saying she was looking to one of the other guests on the ferry as being the murderer, she was hoping it would relax them enough to start implicating themselves. She had been looking for a motive to go along with her suspect, and she believed she had found the match.

"Captain, I was wondering if you had someplace secure where you can place Mr. Hamilton until we reach the dock."

"Yes, ma, I do," the captain said.

Nathan pushed himself back from the table. "What the hell is this?"

A nod from the captain and the tattooed crew member rushed over, placing a beefy hand on each shoulder preventing Nathan from standing.

"Nathan, tell them it's not true," Rose said, leaning somewhat back from her husband.

"Of course it isn't true," Nathan angrily snapped. And to W.W., "You can't just come in here and accuse me of murder."

"Oh, but I have," W.W. said assuredly. "Abby was about to become rich off your basic designs. Ms. Dartley has said she saw your influence in Ms. Growith's work. I don't suppose that set too well with you. You confronted her and she more than likely told you to get lost, or words to that affect, to which your reactions ended with her death."

"It's sheer guess work," Nathan said, his voice elevating as he spoke. "You can't prove any of your hair-brain assumptions."

"I don't have to, Mr. Hamilton, but I suspect the marks on your boot came from the bleach in the storage room, which is all the proof the police will need."

Our next story slips back in time to New York City of the late 1940s, an age when gaslights could still be found in the back streets of outer boroughs, and the neighborhood saloon was the place to find friends, get the news, and maybe hatch a little plan or two ...

Michael Guilebeau tells us the genesis of this story lies in close family history. Recently a finalist for the Silver Falchion, Mr. Guilebeau has received a starred review from the Library Journal for "Josh Whoever", and named it a Mystery Debut of the Month.

Male Leary Comes Home

By Michael Guillebeau

It was darker in the bar than it was on the Bronx docks.

"Mook, when you gonna take down the damned blackout curtains? War's been over three years, nobody tell you?" said Male Leary, coming through the door. He had a heavy sea bag slung over his merchant marine pea coat and a smile on his face.

Mookie looked up from the one beer mug he always seemed to be polishing. He stood over by the cash box, next to the spot where everybody knew he kept his old Army .45. Long as he stood there, fights stayed at a minimum.

"Mr. Leary," he smiled. This was Mookie's second smile of the day, and there was still an hour until closing. Maybe he'd find a third and set a new record. "Back with another made-up story about some bullshit port you say you went to this time?" Mookie asked.

"All true my friend, every word. Particularly this time. Wait until I tell you about West Africa. Won't believe it. Big world out there, Mookie, and I'm going to see it all."

A guy leaning on the scarred-up bar trimming his nails with a switch-blade looked up.

"You Leary?" The guy said. "You don't look like such-a-much to me. Maybe five-eight, not much meat. Don't look more than 25 years old. I expected more."

"I'm a good sailor," said Mr. Leary. "All I want to be. Don't try to be a looker. I know you, pal?"

"No," said the guy, closing the knife, "but my boss knows you." He started to walk out, then turned in the door and said, "And he's looking for you."

"What the hell's that all about, Mookie?" Mr. Leary said after the door banged shut.

Mookie shrugged. "Truck driver thinks he's a wise guy. Seems like, after the war, everybody came back thinking they were wise guys, all the time leaning on more guys to join them."

"Yeah, well, he don't seem too wise to me. Glad I'm out at sea away from this mess." Mr. Leary looked around the bar now that his eyes had adjusted to the dark. There were a few tables and fewer customers all bunched along one side of the dingy room. "No, no, Mookie, you got it all wrong." He started shoving tables around, asking people to stand up and move while he rearranged the room.

An old guy, but a head taller than Mr. Leary stood up grumbling and looked at Mookie. "Mookie, you gonna let him get away with this?"

Mookie had his hand under the bar and just said, "Wait."

Mr. Leary finished. He said, "Here, pal," and seated the old guy at his new spot. "This'll be better on your back." The guy sat down. Mr. Leary turned to Mookie. "See, Mookie, your traffic flow'll be better like this. And you can see the back door better."

Mookie nodded to the old guy. "Mr. Leary comes in every time, rearranges something. Want to shoot him, but when he's done, you stand back and say, yeah, that's better. So I let him. Everybody lets him get away with stuff like that. That's why he's Mr. Leary, at least in this bar. Not Leary, or whatever bullshit first name people make up. Mr. Leary."

"Back does feel better," said the old guy. He raised his glass and Mr. Leary gave him a little salute back.

"See," said Mr. Leary. "Do the job right, take care of problems before they get to be problems."

Mookie waved Mr. Leary over. "Mr. Leary, I want that you should know something. Grimaldi, boss over in Queens, trying to buy Friendly's Restaurant over in College Point. Mr. Friendly don't want to sell. Grimaldi ain't too happy about it."

"Jesus, Mookie, what am I supposed to do? I'm a sailor, not a cop. Two more years, I'll be the youngest captain the merchant fleet's ever seen. I don't belong here on land. Call a cop."

Mookie threw up his hands. "Look, just saying. You rent a room in Friendly's house, like you was family, except that you're also going to marry his daughter Mary. Mr. Friendly just wants to run his restaurant so his friends all have a place to have fun, and Mary has a place to work. Mr. Friendly ain't the kind of guy to stand up to Grimaldi."

Mookie moved down the bar and left Mr. Leary to his thoughts. A few people came and went. Closing time approached before Mr. Leary spoke again.

"Thanks, Mook." "I'll get something set up for Mr. Friendly while I'm back. No idea what, but I'll do something before I ship out again." Mr. Leary set his mug down on the bar and looked up. "Hey, you still got the old Donkey Cart? Think you can run me to the Friendly's? They expect to pick me up at the docks tomorrow. Figure I'll come in now, after they're all asleep, and surprise them in the morning."

Mookie smiled and just nodded. He closed up and led Mr. Leary outside to the Donkey Cart, a 35 Ford coupe with a tarpaper roof. Mr. Leary tried to keep from sticking his hair in the tarpaper as they rode.

They were approaching the Whitestone Bridge into Queens and College Point when something crashed into the back of the Donkey Cart.

"Jesus Christ," said Mr. Leary. He turned in his seat in time to see a truck ram into them again, this time not backing up but trying to push them off the road. "Mook, what the hell?" asked Mr. Leary.

"Some guys don't like me."

Mookie jerked the wheel and the car missed the concrete pillar at the bridge entrance by inches, but he was fighting a losing battle with the truck. The little car edged closer to the side of the bridge.

"Mr. Leary, think of something," said Mookie, fighting the wheel.

"What am I supposed to do? I'm a sailor, not a goddamned magician."

Mookie stomped the gas and pulled away, but the truck caught them again with a bang.

"Mr. Leary, think of something fast."

Mr. Leary reached back for his sea bag.

"Hope you got a gun in there," Mookie said.

"Just souvenirs," said Mr. Leary. "Souvenirs and rocks."

"Don't think they want a post card," said Mookie.

Mr. Leary pulled out a chunk of black volcanic stone and threw it out the window at the truck. It hit the hood and bounced off.

"Mr. Leary, do something now," said Mookie. The front wheel hit the curb and the railing was getting close.

"Last one," he said, pulling out a rock the size of a human head and throwing it at the truck. The truck's windshield shattered when the rock hit it and the truck swerved away and disappeared into the night.

"Mook, what's going on around here? Parts of the Bronx were always tough, but nothing like this ever happened around quiet little College Point," Mr. Leary said as Mookie jerked the car off the bridge and ducked onto the surface streets.

"College Point here is still a small town. Only it sits right between Queens and the Bronx. Bronx mob wants it, Queens, that's Grimaldi, wants it. Getting ugly, particularly if you don't want Bronx or Queens."

"So guys like Mr. Friendly are getting squeezed from both sides. Jesus Christ. Look, I'll talk to the local College Point cops while I'm here. They gotta do something. I can't do nothing when I'm out at sea all the time."

"Cops can't do nothing either. Maybe next time you come back from the sea, instead of serving spaghetti in his own place, Mr. Friendly'll be serving watered-down drinks while some goon watches to keep him in line."

"Yeah." Mr. Leary reached up and picked at a piece of tarpaper, tucking it in so it wouldn't come loose. Mookie thought the conversation was over and let it drop.

After a minute, Mr. Leary looked over at Mookie. "Mook, I can't come back here."

"I know."

"Even when I was growing up," said Mr. Leary, "I didn't belong here. Even how I got my name told me I was nobody. When I was born, Ma told the hospital she'd name me later, so they put down "Male Leary" on the birth certificate. Priest wouldn't baptize me without a name. He rattled off a couple, Ma said, 'Pick one.' He said, 'I baptize you Robert T. Leary.' When I went into the Merchant Marine Academy, I had to show my birth certificate, they said legally I'm Male Leary. Surprise to me."

Mookie just kept driving, giving Mr. Leary time to put the thought together.

"I guess it don't sound like much, but it's kinda like I never had a name here given to me by people who gave a damn. In College Point, I'm just good old Robert T. Legally, I'm some name I never knew I had. But on ship, I'm Mr. Leary, name given to me by men I respect who respect me. I'm somebody there, somebody good. I ain't coming back to some place where I'm just Ma's kid."

"I know."

"'Cept you, Mook. You're the guy who always thought I'd be somebody. Started calling me 'Mr. Leary' back when I was at the academy. But my future's out there on the sea. Nothing back here, excepting Mary."

"Excepting Mary," said Mookie.

"Excepting Mary."

They parked the car on Fourteenth Avenue in College Point and walked down on clean sidewalks with pools of yellow light from the gaslights. Mr. Leary stopped at the window of Friendly's restaurant, next door to the Friendly house, and looked in at the red-checked tablecloths. In the corner, at the back, he saw his and Mary's table. He and Mary talked for hours there while Mary's father took care of the customers so they wouldn't be disturbed. Good to be home.

He noticed a familiar black 1947 Buick parked down the street, but ignored it and went up the steps to the house. He put the key in the door, quiet, and they went in without making any noise. Mr. Friendly was asleep in the big easy chair next to the radio in the parlor. Mr. Leary sat his sea bag down gently and tried not to wake him while Mookie went into the kitchen.

Then he saw that it wasn't Mr. Friendly sitting there with his head slumped down. The man still had his hat on, and there was blood on his shirt. Mr. Leary touched his neck for a pulse, but his skin was cold.

"Jesus Christ," he said softly. He went into the kitchen and told Mookie. They whispered and shrugged for a couple of minutes with Mookie mostly saying, "What are we going to do?" and Mr. Leary mostly saying "Jesus Christ" again. Then Mr. Leary said, "Jeez, Mook, somebody's setting up Mr. Friendly. We gotta get this body out of here." He slung the body over his shoulder and carried it out the back door to the garden shed.

They closed the door to the shed and Mook looked out at the street. "No cops yet."

"Yet," said Mr. Leary.

He went to the refrigerator and picked up two beers and opened them. They went back out the front door and down the street to the Buick.

"Robert T.," said the man at the wheel. The car was new and shiny, but littered with paper coffee cups and waxed paper from take-out hamburgers.

"Here," Mr. Leary handed in the beers. "Thought that was you guys. What's Grimaldi got you boys doing out here? Long ways from Flushing."

The man in the passenger seat had a grin on his face and started to say something, but the driver cut him off with a look.

"Just an errand."

"Tell Grimaldi I said hi. Lot of people in College Point don't like him, but I got no beef with him long as he stays in Flushing."

He turned to walk away. The passenger couldn't keep quiet any longer and said, "What about the surprise? You like the surprise in Friendly's living room?"

Mr. Leary turned and knew he'd guessed right. By morning there would be Queen's cops, owned by Grimaldi, at the Friendly house to arrest Mr. Friendly for the body they'd find.

Mr. Leary looked at Mookie and they both shrugged. "No surprise, boys. Do your job right and nothing ever surprises you."

Mr. Leary leaned in the car's window and looked at the passenger. The passenger wasn't smiling now. He leaned across the driver and stuck his finger in Mr. Leary's face. He started to say something but the driver cut him off.

"Think we'll leave now. Mr. Grimaldi'll want to know you're back."

"Give him my best." Mr. Leary walked back into the house, reached into his sea bag and pulled out a book and a cheap souvenir mask from Africa. By the time he came back out on the porch, the Buick was pulling away. He sat on the porch reading by the light of the streetlight, Mookie sitting in the rocker watching. Soon the Buick returned and stopped across the street. Mr. Leary walked across the street with the mask in his hand, Mookie behind him. Four men got out of the Buick: the two from before and now two more from the back seat. Mr. Leary stopped the men from slamming the doors as they got out.

"Let Mr. Friendly sleep, boys," he said. He turned to an older man dressed in an expensive suit. "Mr. Grimaldi, good to see you."

Grimaldi ignored him and turned to a small, skinny guy and gestured toward the Friendly place.

"That's the house," the skinny guy said, twitching. "In the big chair, living room."

Grimaldi looked at Mr. Leary. Mr. Leary stepped up to Grimaldi, so close his heavy pea coat brushed Grimaldi's suit.

"Nothing in there. Your hired guy here must have made a mistake. Lot of houses look alike down here."

Grimaldi swore.

"Hey, look, Mr. Grimaldi," said Mr. Leary. "I was hoping you'd come by. Brought you this back from Africa." He handed him the mask, but dropped it. Mr. Leary bent down to pick up the mask and came up roughly into the skinny guy. The skinny guy went back against the car and Mr. Leary reached around to steady him. The skinny guy jumped up and pulled a gun.

"Hey," said Mookie.

The gun twitched in the skinny guy's hand, pointing at Mr. Leary's chest.

"Smells like it's been fired," said Mr. Leary, casually. "You ought to clean it after you use it. Man who doesn't respect his tools doesn't respect himself."

He stared at the skinny guy for a long minute. The other two thugs kept their hands in their pockets, waiting. Grimaldi watched Mr. Leary's reaction.

"None of that," Grimaldi finally told the skinny guy. The skinny guy put the gun back in his pocket. Mr. Leary put something in his pocket, too, something he'd taken off the skinny guy.

Mr. Leary shrugged off the incident and smiled at Grimaldi. "Like I said, Mr. Grimaldi, I got you a present. This mask is supposed to protect what's yours. Hang it up in your bar, it'll watch over you." He turned and walked away, said over his shoulder. "May help remind you what's yours and what's not."

"Made a mistake," said Grimaldi, "this time. Maybe next time you'll be out at sea, Leary"

Mookie turned to Grimaldi. "That's Mr. Leary, around here."

The Buick drove away as Mr. Leary and Mookie reached the sidewalk. Mookie went down to Fourteenth Avenue to get the Donkey Cart. They drove into Flushing with the body propped like a passenger in the back seat. Mookie kept to the back streets, nobody out at this hour.

"Jeez, Mook, I'm shaking like a leaf."

"Seemed pretty cool back there with the gunner pointing his piece at you."

"Didn't feel cool on the inside," said Mr. Leary, "but you gotta do it right." He paused. "First time I've had a gun in my face. Three years in the war, a million men trying to kill each other, and I come home to quiet little College Point and find a gun in my face. Jesus Christ."

While they were talking a new sedan with two guys with hats pulled low over their faces eased up next to them at a stoplight. The toughs looked at Mookie and Mr. Leary, Mookie and Mr. Leary looked straight ahead.

"What now, Mr. Leary?" Mookie whispered. "This late, they're either Grimaldi's men or cops. Either way, they find the stiff in the back, we're toast."

"Yeah. Try this, Mook: you look over at them, just a little friendly nod. I'll do this." Mr. Leary turned to the body in the back and started gesturing, like he was explaining something to somebody important. He pointed over at the next car. The men in the car lost interest and the car moved on.

Mookie stopped the Donkey Cart in front of Grimaldi's bar, the bar closed and dark. He and Mr. Leary got out and looked up and down the street a couple of times, like two little kids scared to cross a street for the first time. Mr. Leary stepped back to the car and muttered "C'mon" to Mookie. They dragged the body out of the car and piled it in the doorway, like a bum sleeping it off. Under the body, Mr. Leary put the wallet he'd taken from the skinny guy. They scurried back to the car and pulled away as fast as they could.

"Nice present for the beat cop tomorrow morning," said Mookie as they got back to College Point. "Murder victim, and the wallet of the killer all in one neat package."

"Long as the cop doesn't send us a thank you note."

"But why leave him at Grimaldi's, Mr. Leary? Could have left him in a park, anywhere."

"Send Grimaldi a message: we're here."

The sun was just coming up when Mr. Friendly came downstairs to the smell of fresh African coffee.

"Robert T.," he said. "Son, we're supposed to meet you at the docks this morning."

"Got in early and thought I'd surprise you. How's business?"

"You know, always good. Funny, if you keep a good attitude, just expect things to turn out for the best, they usually do. People are good, and God looks after all of us."

"Yeah," said Mr. Leary. "That's the way it works."

"So I'm the one you came in early to surprise?"

Mr. Leary smiled. "Somebody else live here? About 5'5", red hair, real looker? Heard about somebody like that here."

"Yeah. Surprised she's not up already. She's crazy about you. And she needs somebody like you, somebody to take care of her."

Mr. Leary kept on smiling.

"I know she keeps pushing you to give up sea duty and take a land job," said Mr. Friendly. "She worries about the danger, but I tell her, the guy's a sailor, through and through. You love him, he loves the sea. It's in his blood."

"Yeah."

Mr. Leary stood looking into the living room, past the hand-knitted doilies on the furniture, past the mahogany radio he'd brought back from Italy for Mr. Friendly, through the window to the little gingerbread restaurant next door. To him, it looked like one of those covers on the Saturday Evening Post. Beautiful, but fragile. It wasn't going to last long without help.

Mary came downstairs, already dressed and made up, ready to go to the docks.

"Bob," she screamed and ran to him. She was the only one who called him Bob and Mr. Leary liked it, a name given to him by someone who loved him.

"Hi, Mar," he said, putting out his hand like she was a high school friend he'd seen the day before. She knocked the hand away and grabbed him.

When they broke, she said, "You tell the shipping company you're not going to sail this summer so we can get married?"

"Maybe I better." He looked at her. "Got a friend who knows a guy who needs someone to manage a building down at the gyroscope factory. Think I'm going to take the job, hang around for a while."

"Oh, Bob. That's the answer to my prayers." She dipped her fingers in the holy water font next to the door and crossed herself. "You'll be so much safer."

"Yeah, that's it," said Male Leary. "Safer."

We enter the realm of meta-fiction with our next story. Kate McCorkle gives us a story about a private detective—or is it a story about a story about a private detective? Or perhaps, as all good stories are, it is a story about us.

Ms McCorkle majored in humanities. Her work has been published or is forthcoming in Apiary Online and Diverse Voices Quarterly.

Noir is Dead

by Kate McCorkle

I'd use a hard-boiled metaphor, but that's done for, too. Went the way of the dodo, but—you wouldn't get that either. If you could spell, you could use your thumbs and look it up. You know how to use your thumbs, don't you?

I'm the last of the private dicks: fedora, cigarettes, the works. The Internet destroyed my racket, but there's still occasions that call for a real gumshoe. Time was I'd never take a divorce case. A guy can't afford to be an idealist now. In this scheme, there's the job and then there's the mystery. Rubes think they're the same. They're not.

I was following a lead on Sam the Grocer—owed back payments on a kid. The ex was a cool number who needed the dough. By the looks of her, that wasn't all she needed. She gave me the last known and I headed to the market on Third. Whole Foods. Is there another kind?

Ten feet from the door, a square-jawed lug wearing a green apron told me to put out my cancer stick. I should've taken a stick to him. I pulled my hat down and went for the entrance. A crowd of dames covered their kids' mouths. "Don't inhale!" they screeched, giving me the stink eye. One who left the house without putting on her face shouted that only perverts wore wingtips. Said my kind wasn't welcome there.

Sam knew how to pick a hideout. The place was safer than—oh. Keep forgetting metaphor don't work anymore.

They can't break me from thinking, though. Not yet, anyway.

My feet weren't tired, so I hoofed down Third, past the closed book store, to Mindy's coffee shop. I could use a drink, though I'd prefer rye.

Mindy's customers were under some mind control. Wires coming from their ears, staring at something in their hands no bigger than a deck of cards. No one looked up when I entered. How's a fellow supposed to size someone up if they don't make eye contact? It reminded me of a dope den back in Frisco, but these kids were anything but hard on their luck.

These are the stooges who ended metaphor. Said they already knew everything—didn't need explanation or nuance. If you don't know something you go online; find out what you're supposed to think. So metaphor atrophied and died. The feds wouldn't pay out, and it ended up there.

Funny. You need to live life to make connections and they couldn't cut it. Simile still hangs around. The girls didn't want to give up like. Now only relics like me use metaphor. It's sad, but you won't catch me in a black suit.

The stooges are getting the life they deserve.

No one in this joint can tie a tie or throw a punch, let alone pour a highball. But the clock is ticking and I need to pin down this Sam. The ex thought there was a girlfriend, but it's hard to separate the guys from the dolls. Even when they wear slacks, you can't look for an hourglass; it's comme ci, comme ça. Not even hair helps.

My best bet in Mindy's was a slim brunette, a tall drink of water a few feet away. The hair flips, the hand gestures, the trilling laugh belonged to a dame. I had just put down my drink when she turned. The brunette turned out to be a pock-marked fellow. Face made for radio.

Mindy's shared more with the dope den in Frisco.

The joint was a bust, so I walked up Broad to the library. It was near empty. I grabbed a newspaper and found a club chair that backed up to a bank of computers. A shapely blonde was using one, a duffel at her feet with a green apron spilling out. She moved her chair to make room for me, swiftly kicking the duffel under her seat. I pulled my chair further away.

"You can spread out," I said.

She laughed softly; long fingers moved hair from her eyes. "If it were only that easy," she muttered, returning to her computer.

"You don't look like you have a broken wing."

"Pardon?" She swiveled toward me.

"Sorry. I forgot. You look capable. Empowered. That better?"

"Looks can be deceiving," she muttered, again facing the screen. "But what's it to you? Don't you have a paper to read?"

The doll was talking tough, but she was scared. She couldn't hide the tremor in her voice, the mascara-stained tissue near her hand.

"Look," I said, nudging my chair further away, "I was only trying to be a gentleman. It won't happen again."

"No. I'm sorry," she demurred, turning in her seat to face me. "It's just... oh, I thought I found love, but now I have to find an apartment. I'm supposed to pay support for a kid who's technically not even mine. The court ..." she began to chew her thumbnail. "I'm sorry," she smiled. "You're a stranger, and I'm confessing to you. You probably want to read your paper."

"Name's Bowman," I said, extending my right hand. Her smaller one embraced it.

"Samantha," she said.

"Now we're not strangers, Samantha."

"Guess not. Say ..." she leaned forward. "You know of any apartments for rent? A place where a girl could land on her feet?"

My head snapped up. "What you're saying is dodgy. A guy could get the wrong idea from a lady talking that way."

"You mean a lady with a broken wing?" She leaned closer and lower; the top of her blouse opened; the bauble on her thin gold necklace began to swing.

I took it all in: the jilted lover, the duffel with the green apron, using metaphor on me.

You're good," I chuckled, wagging a finger at her. "You almost had me, Sam. I've been looking for you. Now be a good girl and …

Sam recoiled, eyes blazing. "Carmen sent you, didn't she? Didn't she?"

"So what if Carmen sent me?"

"We could have had something, Bowman. Could have made a go of it. I really do want to land on my feet." Sam wrung her hands.

"I don't know what's real with you. Where's the lie and who's the real Sam?" I threw the newspaper to the floor.

"Landing on my feet was real," she whispered. "I suppose Carmen will find me, now."

I reached in my pocket for a loosey. Sam didn't flinch.

That sealed it.

"It was nice meeting you, Miss," I stood and bowed to Sam, tipping my hat. "Good luck with the apartment." Beautiful Sam and her cares sat at the computer, slack-jawed. The kid would be okay. She would land on her feet.

I left the library without looking back. The wind was heavy; I pulled my collar close. No one walked anymore. I had a wide berth.

⸺⸻•✦•⸻⸺

We now move from grimy back streets to the rarefied air of a penthouse suite, and the requisite murder that the socialite life seems to engender, at least in mysteries.

In David Himmel's work, he explores the ways in which society sets up strata based on wealth and notoriety, and how our personal perceptions of other strata are filtered by our own place on the social ladder.

Mr. Himmel is an author and playwright. He lives in Chicago.

Bravisimo

by David Himmel

In the hierarchy of influence within the philanthropic elite community, Richard and Nancy Denning were the king and queen. They were stalwarts of culture, chairing boards, and financially supporting museums and hospitals, and championing arts programs in public schools.

The Dennings hired Bravisimo, Chicago's most elite catering company, for a party of 50 of their closest and richest friends. The purpose was to introduce their checkbooks to a grand, new effort to stop the gun violence that was killing so many children in Chicago's war-torn south and west sides. The fight for peace in these communities was nothing new, but when local community organizers, the police and the mayor's office couldn't quell the killing, the Dennings saw it time to step in and let the lake-lined Gold Coasters make everything better.

Helping the black and Latino community was not the White Man's Burden, it was the White Man's Privilege.

"Bradley, my darling boy!" Nancy Denning said to me as she walked into her kitchen, which was bustling with two Bravisimo chefs and Mike, the other waiter. I was plating a tray of hors d'oeuvres. "It's been too long!" Nancy Denning was a short woman in her early 70s. Everything about her was calculated for better or worse. From the way she talked, to her perpetual style: her salt-and-pepper bob haircut, her giant black eyeglasses, her colorful scarves that added flair to her otherwise all-black wardrobe. She reached her tiny hands to my face and kissed me on both cheeks like a grandmother. "I'm so happy you were available tonight! Is everything set? How are we on liquor? Do you think I have enough? How's the food? May I try one? What is this?"

"Lime-seared scallop on—"

"Magnificent!" she said, interrupting me with her mouth full. "Our guests should be arriving at any moment. On with the show!" She clapped her hands then whirled out of the room.

"What a loon," said Mike.

"She's sweet," I said.

"All these rich people are full of it. There's not a genuine bone in their bodies. Not unless they bought it."

"They've done more good for this city than you and I will ever do."

"If I had the money, I'd shelter every last homeless person. How about that?"

"I'm sure you would. Why don't you just tend to the bar? You know how these folks like their gin and scotch at the ready. And I noticed that Susie Winston is on the guest list. Make sure there's plenty of Belvedere and soda for her. And lemon—never a lime."

"You're a kiss ass."

Maybe I was. But that's why I was pulling in an average of 60 grand a year, which wasn't bad money for a thirty-three-year-old waiter who worked less than 40 hours a week. I never planned on being a professional waiter, but the money was good when the job market was not. And so, after 10 years working at Bravisimo, I had made a name for myself. The rich wives began requesting me for events because they knew that I would make damn sure that no guest was ever without a drink in one hand and a fifteen dollar-per piece hors d'oeuvres in the other.

The guests started to arrive, mostly two-by-two, like Noah's Ark for moneyed humans. Richard and Nancy Denning circulated through their foyer and front living room making sure to hug and kiss every one. It was shortly after 6 p.m. and I knew that no one had eaten a proper dinner. These people liked to save their appetites for events like these. They loved a free meal and an open bar. I walked around offering scallops and collecting drink orders, while also making polite hellos with the guests, most of whom I knew.

I was passing through the foyer with an empty drink tray when Susie Winston stepped off of the Dennings' private elevator and into their home.

"Bradley!" she said, a smile bursting onto her face.

I sat the empty tray on the table and greeted her with a hug as she kissed my cheek.

"I was beginning to think you were going to stand me up tonight," I said.

"If I had known you were going to be here, I would have made sure to come sooner. I'm so sorry, I was hung up at—Nancy!"

"Susie, my darling girl!" Nancy Denning said.

"I'm sorry I'm late," Susie said. "I was hung up at the hospital. I'm arguing with the board over volunteer programs. It's a crisis. I've been on my feet all day talking to volunteers and patients to get an assessment and prove that a volunteer program is a must. I met the sweetest young woman—a volunteer—she's African-American and lives down by—say, where's Richard? Oh! There he is!"

"Susie, my dear," Richard Denning said as he entered the foyer. A few years older than his wife, he was far less put together than she was. Generally, he looked like a rumpled bag of bones dressed in saggy, but expensive suits. I don't mean this as an insult. He looked around. "Where's Paul?"

"Oh, that husband of mine had some crisis at the office. I swear, it's just crisis after crisis with us." She laughed, charmed with her own melodrama. "Are you sure you want the Winstons involved with you on this project?"

"We wouldn't have it any other way," Nancy Denning said. If the Dennings were king and queen of the philanthropic elite, the Winstons were prince and princess. "Bradley, would you mind taking Mrs. Winston to the bar. I'm sure she could use a drink."

With that, the Dennings were off to make more rounds. I picked up my tray and Susie put her arm in mine as we walked through the kitchen toward the sunroom where the bar was set up. "I made sure to keep a bottle of Belvedere chilled for you," I whispered to her playfully.

"You adorable kitten!" she said.

Susie Winston was a beautiful woman. But then, most rich people are beautiful. It's not that having money makes a person attractive, it's that they can afford to look good, to be healthy, put together, up to date. In her mid-50s, Susie hardly seemed to age a day since I met her a decade before. She was wearing a black skirt that stopped mid-thigh and a cream blazer over a white, silk blouse that was cut just right to do her breasts incredible justice. A small, gold locket hung from her neck and rested at the top of her cleavage. She wore 3-inch black Prada heels that accentuated her toned legs. Her voluminous brown hair bounced with life as she walked and talked and laughed.

After an hour of serving food (the scallops, asian short rib pot pies, lobster and brie purses) and drinks, the Dennings began their spiel.

"And now, ladies and gentlemen! If you'll direct your attention to the center ring ..." Mike mocked.

"Knock it off," I said.

"This is my favorite part. It's where the richer people ask the less rich people for money. They're awful, self-involved megalomaniacs."

"I'm not kidding, Mike. Shut up."

He hunkered down in the kitchen to nibble on the food and sneak a drink or two. I hovered just outside of the living room where Nancy Denning led the presentation. I was interested in what their next charge to change the world was. Contrary to Mike, I didn't think these people were self-involved. Although they had more than plenty of money to give away, they were not selfish with it. Writing a million dollar check was no small gesture no matter how liquid you are.

But, if someone was going to write a check for a million dollars, the events surrounding the cause had better be up to snuff. If the food wasn't right, or the location of the event had bad parking, it could mean leaving

$500,000 on the table. That's why the Dennings were heading up this task. They never missed a beat.

Their home could have been specifically designed to entertain and impress. The considerable living room had several couches, ottomans and cushiony chairs all organized around the fireplace that served as the backdrop to what became the presentation area. Two opposing walls had built in bookshelves stuffed with first editions of classic literature, and world history and American political books and biographies of presidents and scientists. Large windows in the sunroom overlooked Lake Shore Drive and Lake Michigan. When not set up as a bar, it served as a reading room that joined the living room and the dining area of the kitchen, which was the thoroughfare to the foyer and the front door—the private elevator. Down two long hallways on either side of the foyer were the bedrooms, private offices and a bathroom. Just off of the living room was a large formal dining room. The home's floors were marble. The walls were white and where there weren't more built-in bookshelves, there were photographs of small African children. There was only one photo of the Dennings' children and grandchildren. It sat on a windowsill in the dining area of the kitchen. Every other piece of decoration was either a photo of an African child or some colorful African artifact. Africa was very vogue.

Being in the Dennings' home was like being in a comfortable museum. It was clean and airy and well insured.

Nancy Denning talked, but I couldn't take my eyes off of Susie. She was simply stunning that night. And the way the early evening light bathed her as she sat with perfect posture on the edge of a leather ottoman … She made eye contact with me. I pantomimed asking if she wanted a new drink. She smiled, stood up and politely hurried across the room to me. It threw a hiccup into Nancy Denning's so far perfect presentation.

"It's not that I don't care—I do—it's just that I spent two hours on the phone with Nancy last night listening to her rehearse this," Susie whispered to me.

"She's going to talk for two hours?" I said

"God no. I made her whittle it down to 45 minutes—at the most." Susie looked around the room. "Do you suppose people are wondering why the co-chair of this campaign just left the room to come and talk to the gay waiter?"

"Gay?"

"Aren't you?"

"No."

"Oh, my God. I am so sorry. Bradley, I—"

"Why would you think that?" It was a loaded question. I knew exactly why she thought that. The accusation happened often—accusation isn't the right word; that makes it sound like being gay is bad—I was often thought to be gay. I had a fit and clean-cut appearance, never had a long-term girl-friend and I suppose I had a tendency to be expressive with my body when I spoke—I used my hands a lot and shifted my weight. I also flirted with everyone, even the men—just enough to flatter. I had to; flirting is how waiters make their money. The assumption that I was gay was stereotypi-cal bullshit, of course, so I usually ignored it. But it bothered me that Susie thought so.

"I just … Well, I don't know, really," she said. She was clearly mortified by her faux pas because Susie Winston never made a faux pas. "I am so sorry, Bradley. I think I need another drink."

Getting upset wouldn't make a difference. It would only lead to my demotion in this elite group of people. Letting it go meant that it would soon be a silly, private little joke between Susie and I. "Forget about it, I said. "Here, I'll fetch you another drink."

"No, please, let me. I need a moment to collect myself. I'll be right back."

She hurried off to the bar, past Mike who was still sitting in the kitchen, drinking the Dennings' gin. I motioned to him to get up and serve her. He shrugged and gave me a look that said, "Pffssht," before taking a swig of his drink. He watched Susie walk to the bar. He had a good, long look at her ass. I didn't like Mike much, and I loathed his work ethic, but I couldn't blame the guy for gawking. I peeked my head around the corner and watched Susie make a drink. She slugged it back then made another one just as Nancy Denning announced her name to the gathered attendees back in the living room.

"Susie? Susie, darling …" Nancy Denning said.

"I'm here! Sorry," Susie said excusing herself as she squeezed past friends who had formed in the pathway from the sunroom to the living room.

As Nancy lauded the Winstons for their endless good works in this city and their unwavering commitment to this particular campaign, Susie smiled between delicate, but healthy sips of her vodka cocktail. "As many of you know, Susie's husband Paul is usually the one to offer remarks at these sort of things," Nancy Denning said to collective laughter from the audience, who all seemed to understand the joke that Paul was long-winded. "But Paul is hung up at the office, so, Susie, is there anything you'd like to say?"

She gulped down a mouthful of vodka. "Oh, Nancy, I think you've said it all beautifully and perfectly. I suppose, I'd just like to thank all of you for being here and I hope we can count on you to help these poor, terrible children."

The people gasped. Mike, who had come to stand next to me, laughed. Nancy Denning awkwardly put her arm around Susie and said, "I'm sure you don't mean that the children are terrible, but that their situation is terrible."

"Oh, yes. I'm sorry. Of course," Susie said. "Terrible situation." She gave a slight nod of gratitude to the assembled, then turned and leaned down to kiss Nancy Denning on both cheeks before excusing herself. She began walking toward the living room exit where I was standing, but when our eyes met, she looked away, turned around and walked back through the living room to the other side of the apartment like an actor exiting the wrong side of the stage after accepting an Oscar. I watched her disappear down the hallway.

"Piss or puke?" Mike asked me.

"What?"

"Do you think she went to piss or puke? She was looking a little ripped up there."

"I'm sure she's embarrassed and is just going to freshen up."

"Ten-to-one she pukes."

"Go make drinks," I told him.

"She's a hot piece. I bet she likes to get really loaded and screw with nothing but her heels on.

"Jesus Christ, Mike."

"You think I could hit that?"

"Susie Watkins? And you? No. After all, she's married. And if she weren't, you're hardly her type."

"You think you could?"

"Just go make your drinks, Mike."

"I mean, you would, right?"

"Of course I would. And yes, she'd definitely be more apt to sleep with me than you."

"That a challenge?"

"Go."

Nancy Denning concluded the presentation and the socializing resumed. The trick to a good fundraising event is to fill people with alcohol immediately after the presentation. This makes them more willing to write a check right then and there while the warm and fuzzy feelings are still fresh, and their inhibitions reduced.

I had Mike load my tray with the preferred drinks of the big givers I knew Nancy Denning would immediately be asking for a financial commitment that night: Scotch on the rocks for John Herald and a white wine for his wife Lorraine, a white wine for Evelyn Janes, a double gin and tonic for Alan Hughes, a bourbon neat for Steven Bard and a bourbon and ginger for his wife Lucy, and two more glasses of white wine for the Dennings. I delivered the drinks and headed back to the bar to reload with new orders. A line had formed. Mike wasn't there.

"Excuse me," I said to the gatherers. "Where did your bartender go?"

"Don't know," someone said. "I saw him walk down the hall," said another.

"He's probably making an ice run," I said

"Looks like you have plenty of ice," the old and grizzled George Harris said, pointing at the mostly full ice bucket.

"Ah, yes, well … I'll make your drinks," I said. "What'll we have?"

Tending to the bar kept me busy for about 30 minutes before I had time to check the bathroom to see if Mike was hiding out or sick or whatever. I hurried down the nearest hallway to the bathroom and knocked on the door. "Mike?" I said before opening the door. It was empty. I didn't bother to check the other rooms because, although Mike was an asshole, I didn't think he was idiot enough to go playing around in a client's personal areas.

I returned to the living room and was happy to see that the crowd had thinned out. The Dennings were saying their goodbyes and thank yous and collecting a few checks. I heard Alan Hughes slur, "This $200,000 better not go to waste." I felt good knowing that double I served him helped the cause. My self-congratulations didn't last long when I then heard him ask, "Where's Susie? I want to say goodnight to her."

"You know what, Alan, I haven't seen her," Nancy Denning said. "Perhaps she's by the door. You'll see her on your way out."

But Susie wasn't by the door/elevator. In the last 45 minutes, two people had gone missing from the party. But how? The apartment was big, but it wasn't that big. As I made my way through the kitchen to return to the bar, I saw Mike standing there, serving drinks.

"Where were you?" I asked.

"Bathroom."

"I checked the bathroom, you weren't there."

"Well, I was in the bathroom. You must've checked the wrong one." I was in such a frenzy to find Mike that it didn't occur to me to look in the other bathroom down the other hallway. "What's your deal, man?"

"I didn't know where—you can't just leave the bar for a pee break." Mike was pouring another drink for Steven Bard who gave me an odd look when I said this. "Sorry, we've spent years training to hold it," I joked.

"Hey, when a man's gotta piss, a man's gotta piss," Steven Bard said.

"See?" said Mike. "No big deal. I'm back here, pouring drinks. Here, take some white wine out there." He loaded five wine glasses on a tray, filled them up and handed the tray to me. "And quit trying to get me to play hide-and-seek. Slacker."

"Why don't you throw a vodka and soda on here for Susie Winston," I said.

"Oh, I think she left," Mike said.

I was surprised that Susie would leave without saying goodbye. Worried was more like it. Had she embarrassed herself so much that she couldn't face me? What would this mean for my working relationship with her? Public embarrassment was as horrible a thing for the philanthropic elite as dishonoring one's family was for the Japanese. But, unlike the Japanese who would self-sacrifice through hara-kiri, these people would sabotage anyone who was a part of their embarrassment to ensure that the occurrence was forcefully forgotten. I'd seen it happen. A few years ago, William and Beatrice Bedford were the second tier royals above the Winstons. But Beatrice Bedford made an unflattering comment to Susie about Nancy Denning's style, which Susie, of course, mentioned to Nancy Denning, and within a month, the Bedfords were pariahs among their social, philanthropic and business circles. They had to move to San Francisco.

Susie accidentally called the children they were trying to help terrible. She could easily blame that on me, since she had just embarrassed herself after inaccurately assuming I was gay—something she would never admit. If she linked it all to me as the impetus for her flub, it wouldn't take long before she had me fired from Bravisimo. After that, she'd probably ensure that no catering company in the entire state would hire me. I would be ruined. I would have to go back to school.

I had to figure out a way to get a hold of Susie and tell her that her assumption of my homosexuality was completely okay. I just had no idea of how I could actually do it without causing her any further embarrassment or making a fool out of myself. I began to panic just as Richard Denning entered the living room. He had a strange look on his face. "I'm sorry to interrupt everyone's conversations," he said. "But, well ..." He looked down, then at his wife who looked confused and annoyed, then back down the hallway from which he came, then at no one in particular in the living room. "I'm just curious ... Can anyone tell me why Susie Winston is naked and dead in my and Nancy's bedroom?"

The few remaining friends gasped with the same energy as they had when Susie called the kids terrible. I didn't think I heard him right so I said, "What?"

"Yes, well, it seems that Susie's head was smashed in with the lamp from my nightstand," Richard Denning said. More gasps.

"You sure she's dead?" Steven Bard said.

"Well, Steven, she's not moving and there's quite a bit of blood."

"And she's naked?" asked Evelyn Janes.

"Yes, it seems so," said Richard Denning.

"Is there blood on the carpet?" she asked.

"Yes, I'd say a fair amount."

Nancy Denning let out a desperate, "No!" before fainting. I dropped my tray and caught her just as the glasses I'd been carrying shattered on the marble floor. George Harris helped me carry her to the couch.

"We should call the police," said Lucy Bard.

"We should have a look in the room," John Herald said. His wife Lorraine smacked him in the arm.

They all filed down the hallway to see Susie. I was left with Nancy Denning's tiny head in my lap. Mike and the two chefs had come out to the living room to see what was going on. The chefs followed the crowd to the room. Mike asked me if I wanted a cold towel for Nancy Denning.

"Please," I said.

"So, who died?" he asked me when he returned a moment later.

I patted the towel on Nancy Denning's face and forehead. "Susie Winston. I thought you saw her leave."

"I didn't know that's who you were talking about."

"When you came back from the bathroom, I asked you to make a vodka-soda for her and you said she already left."

"Well, of course she didn't leave, man. She was dead." He laughed.

"You're a sick bastard." He just shrugged.

Nancy Denning began to come to. She looked up at me. "Is it true? Is Susie?"

"Yes. I guess. I don't know. I haven't seen anything."

"We must go look."

She slowly sat up and we walked to the bedroom. Mike stayed back. "Start cleaning up," I told him. "I'll send the chefs back, too." He shrugged again.

———

I was ashamed of myself for thinking that Susie looked gorgeous laying naked on that bed despite her brains spilling onto the floor. But then, it's really quite the compliment, isn't it? It was a beautiful death scene. Like one that had been staged for a photo shoot commissioned for hundreds of thousands of dollars by one of these philanthropists to raise money for the Museum of Contemporary Art. The blood was thick and was drained from her broken skull. The rest of her body seemed untouched. Her heels were still on her feet. Her eyes were open and stared at the ceiling. Her mouth was frozen in a small smile. Other than Susie's shattered head and the lamp on the floor, nothing was out of place. Not the dozen pillows on the Dennings' California king bed, not the comforter or the sheets, nothing.

"Oh, Susie," Nancy Denning said as she approached the bed. She reached out to touch her dead friend's hand.

"Nancy, don't! This is a crime scene," said Lucy Bard. "We really should call the police."

"Was she raped?" asked John Herald.

"Is that what you want?" Lorraine Herald barked at him.

"No. I'm just wondering if that's why she's naked."

"She was so beautiful," Evelyn Janes said.

"I think we should all go and leave the woman in peace. Let the authorities sort this mess out," Lucy Bard said.

"I don't know if that's a good idea," Richard Denning said. "The police will probably want to question those of us at the party."

"Like any of us did it?" George Harris said, offended.

"No, George. To find out if any of us saw anything," Lucy Bard said.

"But so many people already left," John Herald said. "The person who did this could already be gone. Who was the last person Susie was with?"

"I saw her talking to him," Evelyn Janes said pointing at me.

"I didn't do this," I said.

"Prove it!" she said.

"I was out in the living room serving food and drinks all night."

"It's true," Richard Denning said. "Bradley could not have done this."

"I saw him walk down the hallway when his other waiter pal went missing," said George Harris. "But, I suppose that was hardly enough time to screw and kill someone."

"Unless he's a two-pump-chump," Steven Bard said to everyone's disgust. "All right, all right," he said. "Well, what were you doing in the hallway?" He gestured quotation marks with his fingers when he said the word hallway.

"I was looking for Mike, the other—Holy shit!" I ran out of the room, through the hallway to the kitchen where the chefs were nearly through cleaning up. Mike was gone.

"Where'd he go?" I asked them.

"Cleaned up the bar. Asked if he could go. Told him sure, we'd load everything in the truck. No problem," the taller chef said.

"Goddammit." I pulled my phone out and called Mike. He didn't answer. I left him a message that he needed to come back to avoid any potential suspicion. "Don't leave," I told the chefs. We all need to stay here until the cops come."

"Is there really a dead women back there?" the shorter one asked.

"Yes," I said.

"Naked?"

"Yes," I said. I became incredibly suspicious. The chefs were the only two people I hadn't paid any attention to all night. "Did you kill her?" The short one shook his head. "Did you?" I asked the taller one. He also shook his head. "I'm sorry. Of course not. Okay, just, stay here—don't touch anything."

"Should we finish cleaning up," the short one asked me.

"No. Not yet. Leave everything where it is. We don't want to contaminate any potential, um, clues, or whatever."

Everyone was still gathered around the bed looking at Susie. Despite the seriousness of the situation, the philanthropists had begun the usual end-of-the-evening gossip. However, instead of it being about who wore what, said what or didn't write a big enough check, these friends of Susie's were attaching motives for murder to each guest not standing in that room at that moment. You'd never heard trash talking like this.

"I told my people to stay," I interrupted. "But Mike, the man bartending tonight, he left. I called him and left him a message, Hopefully he'll come back. I'm sure he didn't do this, but I want you to know, Mr. and Mrs. Denning, that I will personally see to it that the police speak with him. Has anyone called the police yet?" I looked at Susie's body. The blood had stopped pooling. Her body was gray. The once picturesque scene finally revealed itself as a crime scene. Death had become more obvious now than the beautiful, naked woman lying spread eagle and smiling on what must have been a $2,000 comforter.

"Lucy, dear, were you going to call them?" Richard Denning said. "If you do, please don't use our name. Simply use our address and unit number—it's unit 13—"

"That explains it," Steven Bard said. Everyone looked at him. The stares demanded an explanation. "This is the thirteenth floor. That's bad luck."

"Oh, would you just shut up, Steven," his wife Lucy said.

"Unit 13," Richard Denning continued. "Tell the 9-1-1 dispatcher that someone has been injured at a small, private gathering. I'll call down to the doorman and let him know we're expecting some police to investigate a potential robbery. Someone stole some of Nancy's jewels."

"What'll you tell them when the coroner comes up and then carries a body out of the front door?" said John Herald.

"Well, John, the thing is that … I don't want any attention being drawn to this. It could become a great scandal because of who we all are and who Susie is—was—and most importantly, it could affect fundraising for our campaign. We're trying to stop murders in this city. The idea that a murder occurred during our first fundraiser will not make a good impression on the public or our donor base. I also don't want to alarm any of the other residents. The last thing Nancy and I need is the Building Association getting up in arms over a murder.

"We'll have to explain to the Association why we're getting new carpeting in the bedroom," Nancy Denning said.

"We'll say that one of the grandkids spilled grape juice."

Lucy took her phone out of her small purse. "Now wait a minute," George Harris said. "This is getting too complicated. Lucy, put the phone down. We're not calling 9-1-1. This isn't an emergency. We have a dead woman on our hands and murderer who needs to be brought to justice. Uniformed flatfoots aren't going to do a thing, and that's who the 9-1-1 operator will send over. Then they'll radio for the homicide detectives and coroner and clean-up units and all of that to come by. If we report this to the bottom of the totem pole, we're going to get the whole goddamn police force involved, and like Richard is getting at, there's just no reason for it."

"What are you saying, George?" Nancy Denning asked.

"I've got a guy. He used to work in the homicide department. He's an old friend. He's real good about keeping things as quiet as possible. Look, there's no way this is going away. This is Susie Winston we're talking about here. It's not like someone killed that waiter kid." He gestured to me. "But my guy can help. I'll call him. Give me a few minutes."

George Harris left the room. The rest of us stood there in silence. The more I thought about what he said about had I been the victim, the more I began feeling nervous. I wasn't one of these people. They couldn't trust me to not talk. Of course I wouldn't, but they would never take my word for it. They could easily have me killed and make it so no investigation would ever be conducted. It'd be easy to do. My family wouldn't file a missing persons report—they never saw me anyway. Bravisimo might, but probably not. Their concern of my whereabouts might only arise when I wasn't around to meet requests or when the busy holiday season arrived. I was a part of the Bravisimo Family, sure, but work-based families are only as strong as your availability to show up and clock in.

When George Harris returned, he had a smug look on his face. "It's all set. My guy will be here shortly."

We made our way to the living room to wait. Upon Richard Denning's request, I opened a bottle of The Glenlivet 21 from his private scotch collection. He wasn't a big drinker, but he stockpiled the good stuff for special occasions. Susie Winston being murdered on his bed was one such occasion. We all drank in silence. Richard Denning even invited the two chefs to imbibe.

George Harris' guy showed up 20 minutes later. The man was short and stocky. He had slicked back gray hair underneath a black fedora. Although it was early summer, he was wearing a black leather jacket and matching gloves. He had a strong, south side Chicago accent. I wasn't sure if his appearance and attitude were a result of being a cop for so long or if he became a cop because of his appearance and attitude.

"I'm sorry you're having trouble tonight," he said to the Dennings as he removed his hat. "Can I see the victim?" Richard and Nancy Denning escorted him to the bedroom. The rest of us followed.

He handed his hat to George Harris. "Thanks, Georgie," he said. He looked around the room. Then he walked around with what seemed to be no particular purpose. When he got to the opposite side of the bed from where we stood—the side where the bloody lamp lay on the floor—he said, "First thing: My name isn't important. What's important is that we keep this delicate situation under as much control as possible without obstructing justice and making damn sure we find the perpetrator of this crime."

"Are you even a real police officer?" Lucy Bard asked.

"Ma'am, I've been working with the Chicago Police Department since old man Daley was boss. If you're concerned about my ability, or my legitimacy, don't be. If you're concerned that I don't do things by the book, you don't gotta worry about that neither."

"I just think it's best if …"

"She your wife?" the man asked Steven Bard.

"Yes."

"Get her outta here. She's trouble. We got enough trouble. I don't need a lippy trophy wife causing more of it."

Lucy Bard huffed and puffed to her husband as he led her out of the room. I felt the tension increase as everyone became afraid of upsetting the man who was there to fix things.

"What was this woman wearing when she first arrived?" the man asked no one in particular. When no one in particular didn't speak up, I did.

"White blouse. Black skirt. High heels. A cream blazer."

"Who're you?" the man said.

"He's the waiter, Bradley," Nancy Denning said.

"How'd you know so much about what she's wearing?" he said as he stepped closer to me. It was an intimidation technique and it was working.

"He's a homosexual. He is well aware of women's fashion," Nancy Denning said.

"No, I'm not gay." I said.

"You're not?" she said with surprise. "Oh, my, God. I'm so sorry, Bradley."

"I thought he was gay, too," Evelyn Janes said.

"Can we let the man get on with it?" John Herald said.

"Well," said the man. "How'd you know so much about what she was wearing?"

"Because I always thought Susie—um, Mrs. Winston—looked so well dressed and, um, put together."

"You find her attractive?"

"Uh, sure."

"But you wouldn't screw her and kill her, would you?"

"What? No!"

"Bradley would never, sir," Nancy Denning said. "We've all known Bradley for years. He coordinates and manages many of our events and parties. Susie always spoke very highly of him." That made me feel good.

"Maybe you don't know him so well. A minute ago, you thought he was gay. She ever think you were gay? Ask you about it?" the man said to me as he gestured to Susie's body.

"Once," I said. But "Oh, shit," is what I thought.

"Yeah? When?"

"Tonight, actually."

"That upset you?"

"Not really. I get it a lot."

He took a step back and looked at me. "Yeah, I could see that. Mrs. And Mrs. Denning, you knew each and every guest who was here tonight?"

"Of course. Everyone in attendance was a personal friend of ours. And of Susie and her husband," Nancy Denning said.

"No one snuck in?"

"No."

"I'm going to need a list of all the people who were here. And I want all of us to go down that list and consider any potential motives or opportunities anyone may have had to hurt the victim. I also want to speak to each of you here now about the victim's actions tonight. You say she's got a husband? Where is he? Was he here tonight?"

"No," Nancy Denning said. "He was supposed to be, but Susie said he was hung up at the office."

The man seemed satisfied with that answer and went back to Susie's body to get a closer look at her wound and the lamp.

"There's no obvious signs of any kind of struggle," the man said. "Without a rape kit, I can't tell for certain if there was any actual sex that occurred, although her lipstick looks a little smudged, like maybe she was kissing somebody. Her shoes are still on. Makes me think there was some sexual urgency. You know how some men like to screw women with their heels still on." George Harris and John Herald both chuckled knowingly. Lorraine Herald looked embarrassed.

Susie looked more like a corpse every moment. I looked over her naked body and compared it against all the times I imagined her naked. I closed my eyes and shook the perversion from my head. And then I knew that something was missing. Richard Denning's earlier plan to disguise the murder as a robbery in the initial police report was not entirely wrong.

"What about her necklace?" I said. Everyone looked at me strangely.

"What necklace?" the man asked.

"I remember that she was wearing a small, gold locket tonight. She's not wearing it now." Everyone in the room looked at the floor and shifted like vat of acid had just been dumped at their feet.

The man approached me again. He got right in my face as best he could—considering he was a good six-inches shorter than me—and sized me up. "You sure you're not a homo?"

"I'm sure," I said. "The necklace stood out to me because it, well, it complimented her, you know, her chest."

"Kid's not gay," George Harris said, "He's a pervert."

"No, no, Georgie," his guy said. "The vic was clearly a nice looking lady. Can't blame the kid. Now, everyone stand right where you are, I'm going to move some things around and see if we can find this necklace. What'd you say it looked like?"

"A small, gold locket," I said.

The man gently lifted Susie's head just enough to see if the locket was underneath it. Nothing. He gently rolled her body over lifting her shoulder and back off the mattress. Nothing. He looked in the pillows. Nothing. He looked under the bed, behind the bed, under and behind the nightstands. Nothing. He looked through her clothes near me at the foot of the bed. Nothing.

"The perp must've taken it," the man said. "When I get my guys up here, we'll take a better look, but I'll bet my last dollar that he took it as a trophy."

"Why wouldn't he take her wedding ring, too?" Evelyn Janes asked.

"Murders aren't necessarily thieves," the man said. "Taking a trophy isn't about robbery."

Just then, Steven Bard walked in the room. "I'm sorry to interrupt, but Paul is here."

"Who's Paul?" said the man.

"Did anyone call him?" Nancy Denning asked. Everyone looked around expecting someone else to say, "Yes, I called Susie's husband and told him his wife is dead." No one did. "Damnit!" Nancy Denning said, much to the surprise of everyone, including herself.

She led the charge to the living room to meet Paul. We all followed like the voyeurs we had become. All of us except George Harris' man.

"Oh, Paul," Nancy Denning said as she hugged him. "I'm so sorry."

"I'm the one who should be sorry, Nancy. I'm terribly late. I didn't know if the evening would still be carrying on. I called Susie several times but she never answered, so I thought it best to just pop on over. Where is Susie?"

"Paul, my boy …" Richard Denning started.

"And can anyone tell me why I found her locket on the sidewalk just outside of the building?"

We gasped. Again.

"Paul," Richard Denning continued. "Susie, it seems, has been, well, she has been murdered."

"Excuse me?" Paul Winston dropped onto a chair. I grabbed the bottle of scotch we'd been drinking from and handed him a glass of it. "My God," he barely whispered. He emptied the glass in one gulp. He looked at the locket in his hand. "But how did the locket get outside?"

"We just noticed it was missing. Maybe the person who did this dropped it on his way out," Richard Denning said.

"You let the murderer leave?" Paul Winston said furiously.

"No, no, Paul, darling. We didn't know she was killed until the end of the evening. No one has left since," Nancy Denning said, trying to reassure him.

"That other waiter left," Lucy Bard said.

"Thank you, Lucy," Nancy Denning said curtly.

"What kind of party are you people throwing here? Where are the police? What is going on?" Paul Winston said, tears falling from his eyes.

George Harris' guy emerged from the hallway and entered the living room. He held a wine key by a handkerchief in his hand. He held it up as a display to everyone in the room. Another collective gasp.

"Let me ask you, waiter," the man said. "You use these often?"

"Of course," I said as my stomach did summersaults in my throat.

"You usually carry one around with you, say, on your person when working?"

"Usually."

"You got one with you tonight?"

"Sure." I reached into my back pocket where I kept my wine key. It wasn't there.

"What's the matter? Missing something?"

I didn't know what to say or do. Everyone was staring at me. I couldn't tell if they were angry or confused. Paul Winston stood up and stepped toward me.

"You goddamn sonofabitch," he said raising the scotch glass.

I closed my eyes and prepared myself to be smashed in the head just like Susie. For a moment, I felt close to her. Then I remembered what happened to my wine key.

"It's on the bar!" I said.

Paul relaxed.

"What's that?" the man said.

"I left my wine key on the bar when I was bartending after Mike went to the bathroom."

"What the hell is a wine key?"

"That. The bottle opener." I headed for the bar, but stopped when I saw, and remembered, that Mike broke everything down. I quickly rummaged through the kitchen on the chance that he packed the wine key up with everything else. It wasn't there.

"Kid, you're going to have to come with me," the man said. He pulled out a pair of handcuffs. "You have the right to remain silent ..."

"No, no! This isn't right. I left mine on the bar when Mike was gone—he must've done this! That's his wine key!"

"Oh, Bradley, how could you?" Nancy Denning said.

George Harris was holding Paul Winston back from beating my face in. The man grabbed me, turned me around and placed the cuffs on my wrists.

"This isn't right!" I shouted. "You need to be looking for Mike."

"Maybe we do," the man said. "But right now, you're the prime suspect."

"Is this even legal? Let me see your badge. You're not done reading me my rights. I couldn't have done this, I was working the whole time!"

"Mr. and Mrs. Denning, I'm going to call this one in and have my special team come here tonight and have the victim removed and your home dusted for prints and what-not. We'll build a good case for the lawyers to punish this deviant." As he led me out of the apartment, he yanked on my cuffs, which pulled me into him. "All this just 'cuz she thought you were gay," he said to me.

As we approached the apartment's elevator, my phone rang. "Wait!" I said. "It could be Mike. Please, let me answer it." The man pulled my cell phone from my front pocket.

"It says it's Mike Cartwright. That the guy?"

"Yes!" The man tried to answer it but his leather gloves wouldn't work with the touch screen. Frustrated, he handed it to Richard Denning who slid his finger across it, put it on speaker and held it up to my face. "Mike? Mike!"

"Hey, Brad. You still at the Dennings'?"

"Yes!"

"Great. I just got home and realized that I accidentally grabbed your wine key when I left. I lost mine somewhere. If you see it, can you grab it for me?"

"No shit you left it here, you bastard!" I shouted into the phone.

"Whoa, whoa, man. Relax. You're too high-strung. You have to learn to take it easy. You'll get yourself in trouble some day."

"You sonofabitch. Come back here and tell these people that it's your wine key and that you killed—"

"So, you found it? Where was it? Oh, that's right, I left it in the room with that dead lady. Enjoy the rest of your night, Brad."

We travel now to the small, and possibly forgotten, town of Nameless, Texas, in a story by prolific Bobbi A. Chukran. Ms Chukran's writing encompasses a novel, novellas, short stories, essays, plays, how-to books, and more.

In this story, a young man is about to discover that most ancient of admonishments, stay away from loose women.

So, pour yourself a cold one, cue the honky-tonk piano, and settle yourself in for a story of Cozy-Noir, told Texas-style.

Dead Dames Don't Wear Diamonds
A "Nameless, Texas" Noir Short Story

by Bobbi A. Chukran

I wonder how many damned fools have been led astray by a blue-eyed buxom blonde whispering the simple phrase through her blood-red lips, "All you have to do is …"

Fill in the blanks. Whether it's "All you have to do is kill my husband for me and I'm yours." Or "All you have to do is steal this money for me and I'm yours." It doesn't matter.

All I can say is, I'm one of those damned fools. In my case, it was "All you have to do is steal some documents from the safe in my husband's office and I'm yours." And of course, I fell for it. And that was all it took.

I tell you, I'm in a lonely place right now. All I have is time to try and figure out how everything went wrong.

Way it happened, how I first met her, she was sitting in a back booth in Do-Lolly's Diner, sobbing her eyes out. It was late, nobody else was in there, so I walked over to her, handed her a clean handkerchief and asked if there was anything I could do to help.

She looked up at me, sniffed, dabbed at her eyes, and indicated that I should sit down. "Buy me a cup of coffee?" she said, with a tremulous smile.

"That depends," I said. "I might, if you tell me your name."

"Billie," she said. "Billie Burkett."

I'd seen her around town, but couldn't place her at first. She was one fine woman, all dressed up, her hair and face fixed like she was out on the town. She wore boots made of hand-tooled leather with some intricate stitching up the sides. She wore a skimpy tube top thing with a filmy white shirt over it, her tiny waist cinched in with a wide leather belt that also had some fancy stitching and an etched silver belt-buckle with a big hunk of turquoise in the middle. She wore a short denim skirt that had some kind of ruffle around the edge. Around her neck, she wore a matching turquoise and silver squash-blossom necklace that must have weighed five pounds.

My ex- used to call this style of clothing the "Southwest slut" look. I knew she was wearing at least five-thousand dollars worth of western wear. Not that I didn't admire it. Truth be told, I wish more Texas women would dress like she did.

"What seems to be the problem, little lady?" I asked, doing my best John Wayne. That never fails to get a smile from the ladies.

Well, almost never.

She sighed. "I'm stuck here in god-forsaken Nameless, Texas, of all places, in a loveless marriage."

"Oh, is that all?" I joked. And finally, she gave me a little smile.

"I'm no nun," she continued with another big sigh. "Tee-Bone spends all his time at work and has no time for me anymore. He spends all his time down at that filthy, stinky bar of his."

Ah, yes. Tee-Bone. Tee-Bone Burkett, the owner of the Blue Orchid. The Orchid was a little dive bar down near the river. It attracted the biker crowd, the rowdy outlaw types.

"So you're Tee-Bone's wife?" I asked. I seemed to remember seeing her down at the Orchid the few times I've been in there. It wasn't really my kinda place but I'd been there a time or two for happy hour. I took another look at her necklace nestled in between her breasts and had to wonder how a bar-owner's wife could afford such fancy attire.

"You're trouble; that's easy to see," I tried joking again.

She tossed her long blonde curls over her shoulder. "Yeah, what of it? I'll admit that I'm poison, to myself and everybody else. But that's just part of my charm. I'm the bad girl all the guys want to..." She stopped and took a puff of her cigarette. She blew out the smoke slowly, and my gaze was focused on her lips.

I gulped, and then asked, "To what?"

"To be with."

A raging torrent of emotion ripped through me, and I was totally undone. At that moment, I would have thrown myself off the edge of the Grand Canyon for that dame. And like a fool, I opened up my trap and said, "What do I have to do to … be with you?" I gulped, blushing.

"Well, aren't you the sweetest thang," she cooed, then slithered over in the booth, pulling me down beside her. She squeezed my arm and her nails were long and blood red. She gave me a long look up and down, her eyes halting just a moment on my belt buckle. It was a really big one, and I'm proud of it. I'd won it for bull riding at the county rodeo.

"So, cowboy. What is your name, by the way?"

"My name is Dan. Dan Taylor."

"Well, pleased to meet you, Dan Taylor," she said. "I haven't seen you around here before."

I explained that I had grown up in Nameless, but had been out of town for a few years. I didn't elaborate further, but she didn't seem to notice. Or she didn't care.

"I'll bet you're dynamite with a gun or a girl," she said.

"A gun?"

"By the way, do you own a gun?"

"Sure, why do you ask?"

She shrugged. "Just curious. Seems like everyone in this town has at least one that they'll admit to. Can't a girl be a little curious about a guy she's going to …?"

"Going to what?" I grinned. "Be with?"

She smiled mysteriously. "Going to go to dinner with. Buy me dinner, all right? We can talk about our future together."

"Sure, I'll buy you dinner." I reached over for the menu, then she put her hand on mine and her long nails pressed into the back of my hand. My breath hitched in my chest and I looked up into her blue eyes.

"Not here, not in this dump. Someplace nice. Someplace special, all right?" she said.

I almost pinched myself to see if I was dreaming. It was very seldom that a woman this beautiful gave me the time of day.

OK, not seldom—think never.

Then I came to my senses. "What about your husband? Won't he object?"

She smiled. "He lets me have friends, and we go to dinner occasionally. Besides, he's at that damned bar all the time; he'll never miss me."

I looked her over. "A fine woman like you? Well, that's a damn shame. I'd be honored to take you to dinner. Just name the place."

She named a little out-of-the-way restaurant in the Hill Country on the outskirts of Austin. It was about 25-miles away, so I was fairly sure that nobody would recognize us there.

Not that we were doing anything wrong. But tongues do wag in small towns, and I'd just as soon not get on Tee-Bone's bad side.

We made arrangements to meet the next night, and I grinned like an idiot all the way home.

I stayed with my Aunt Gilda for a while, until I could find a place of my own. She's okay, not like most old broads her age. She's Texas-tough and doesn't take guff from nobody. She watched over me like a mother hawk at times, but pretty much let me do what I wanted as long as I didn't get drunk and wreck the house. She lived in an old house near downtown Nameless and I earned my keep by fixing things for her. There was always something that needed to be fixed in an old house like that.

I finally crawled out of bed around 11 a.m., drank some coffee and spent most of the day washing and waxing my truck. I wanted it to look nice for my date with Billie.

I spent about as much time getting myself ready, and took extra care with my clothes and found some old Brut aftershave that had been my uncle's before he passed away. I took a whiff of it, shrugged, and then splashed on a copious amount.

I was antsy, hung around the house like a moony hound dog the rest of the day until time to leave. I wanted to sneak out without Aunt Gilda seeing me, but unfortunately, she was sitting right smack in front of the back kitchen door, so I couldn't avoid her.

Aunt Gilda loved painting on velvet. She was sitting at the kitchen table, mumbling as she painted. Her current masterpiece was a single flower, in blue. I stopped for a moment, squinted at it and said, "Is that an orchid? It sure is pretty."

"No, Dan, it's a dahlia, dammit," she said, a bit miffed that I didn't recognize it. She put a few more dabs on the picture, then threw down the brush and wiped her hands on her apron. "I'm tired of painting anyway." She grabbed her knitting bag from the floor, took out a ball of pink yarn and something shaped like a little hat.

"Is that a hat for Sister's new baby?" I asked, trying to make amends.

"No, idiot child, it's a tea cozy. A knitted tea cozy."

Oh, I see. I thought it better to quit asking questions at that point.

She knitted for a few seconds then threw the wad down on the table. "I hate knitting," she said. "Everybody thinks I should knit because I'm over the age of 65, and that sucks." She cocked an eye at me.

"You look nice," she said, finally noticing my string tie, pressed jeans, long-sleeved white shirt and ostrich-skin boots. "Where are you going?"

"Out on a date."

"Well, glory be! It's about time you got out and about. Who are you going with, anybody I know?"

"Just somebody I met."

"Where'd you meet her?" she asked.

I blew out a breath. Just get it over with. "I met her down at Do-Lolly's Diner last night. Her name is Billie."

She gave me that look then she went stone cold still. "Not Billie Burkett, I hope!"

"Yes, Billie Burkett. We're just friends," I said, squirming a bit.

"Oh, my lord! You don't have the brains God gave a goose! You stay away from her! That woman is an amoral black widow spider, an evil hussy, and a home-wrecker, to boot."

"Are we talking about the same woman?"

"She's a fallen angel, that one. I remember when she was younger, used to sing in the choir, but then she seduced poor Pastor What's-His-Face, stole all his money, and hit the road." She stopped to take a breath. "Poor preacher's wife has never been the same since." She shook her head.

"Oh yeah, and she's an ice-pick murderess, to boot." She frowned, and then mumbled, "Allegedly."

I stared at my aunt. Surely she was thinking of someone else.

"She finally slunk back home and married that bar owner, what's his name?" she continued. "Boy, those two are a pair!"

She can't be all bad, I thought. Surely my aunt was mistaken. Her memory wasn't what it used to be.

"I can take care of myself," I said, and in the back of my mind I hoped it was true. I admit I was nervous about going out with such a beautiful babe. I pushed thoughts about her husband to the back of my mind.

As I walked out the back door, I heard the phone ring, and I hesitated as Aunt Gilda went to answer it. "Sorry, you have the wrong number," I heard her say. Glad for the distraction, I pulled the door firmly shut as I went off into the night, whistling a sad little tune.

I couldn't get it out of my head and I couldn't place it, but I knew it was from some old movie. I knew it would come to me eventually.

———————

Billie was dressed to kill when I picked her up later that night. She wore the same boots she'd had on the night before, but this time she wore a dress that made my eyes pop right out of my head like in some old cartoon. It was made of black velvet with long, black see-through lace sleeves. It skimmed the top of her boots at the hem. She wore a huge necklace type thing about the size of a Buick, made up of strands of turquoise beads and leather lacing all twined together. Over this, she wore a short little faded jeans jacket with silver buttons.

I thought she was a bit overdressed for the Mockingbird Inn, but I didn't want to spoil the mood. She frowned when she saw my truck, but quickly recovered and I helped her up into the cab. We talked a bit on the drive to the Inn, but mostly we just hummed to oldies on the radio. We had similar tastes in music. She said she liked George Jones, Tammy Wynette, Loretta Lynn. I thought that was a good sign. After a while, she loosened up and even laughed at a few of my jokes.

Heads turned as we walked in, and I couldn't help but be thrilled at the attention. It wasn't often that I took out a woman like Billie Burkett.

Dinner went well, and I almost had a coronary when I saw the prices on the menu but didn't want her to think I was a heel. Billie ordered grilled lobster and talked me into getting a bottle of champagne. Luckily, I had Aunt Gilda's credit card that I was supposed to be using for groceries and such. I'd pay her back when I got a job.

By the time there was nothing left of the champagne but a few bubbles in the bottom of the bottle, we were quite friendly with each other and she led me to believe that I'd be spending the night in her bed.

I was almost right. We didn't go to her house. We ended up at the Cactus Court Motel, a quaint little place not far from Nameless. It's definitely not the Hilton, but it is clean, and we were able to get a room in the back, off the highway. Billie didn't seem to mind. I was glad it was late at night. One of my aunt's friends owns the place, and I didn't want to be seen. News can get from one end of Nameless to the other in about five minutes these days, now that everybody's granny and their dog has a cell phone.

I locked the door and pulled her into my arms. She kissed me, then gently pushed me away. "There's just one little thing I need you to do for me first," she purred as she slid her hand up my thigh and squeezed. "Then we can both have what we want."

"Anything, name it," I said, running my hands through her hair. I couldn't believe my luck.

She pulled away and smiled. "I just need you to get some documents for me. They're in the safe, in a back room in the bar office."

"What kind of documents?" I asked.

She shrugged. "Nothing much of importance. Just some insurance stuff—papers, mostly. Tee-Bone wouldn't let me read the policy on the bar and I think I have a right to see it."

I readily agreed to do it. What harm would it do? After all, how much trouble could I get into for doing a little safe-cracking? It's not like it would be the first time.

Our first night together was indescribable. When I woke up the next morning, I reached out for her, but she was gone. I had no idea how she got home.

———••———

I waited close to three in the morning, until I knew everybody had left the bar. Billie gave me a key, so I didn't have any trouble with the back door. The alarm only went off if somebody tried to break in without a key, so that wasn't an issue. Once in, I stumbled around in the dark for a bit, found the office, and the safe.

I had no trouble getting into the safe. The lock on it was only a formality, and within a few minutes I had the door open and reached inside. I found a small stack of cash, which I left behind, and a big thick heavy envelope that obviously had papers in it. But there was something else too, a small packet. I slipped the packet inside the envelope. I heard a car door slam out in front, so I grabbed the packet, pushed the safe door shut and ran through the back door, just in the nick of time.

The next morning I called her. "I got it," I said into the phone. She seemed distracted and there were voices in the background, some muted laughter.

"Should I come over now? I can bring the stuff."

"No! Let's meet later, after dark," she said. "I have a few things I need to do first. Oh, and Dan, don't look in the envelope, all right?"

I agreed, although of course I was curious.

She finally called and asked me to meet her at the bar. I hesitated, but she said it would be safe. Tee-Bone had gone to Austin to the bank and wouldn't be back for several hours. The bartender, Curly McCloud, was a friend of hers, she said, and could be discreet when motivated.

She was already there when I arrived, sitting in a back booth. I slid over into the seat across from her, and handed her the envelope and she smiled. She snatched the envelope out of my hands, opened it, taking out some papers. Then she took a smaller envelope out of the larger one. She opened it up and poured at least a dozen sparkling diamonds into her hand.

I gulped. Diamonds? "I thought you said those were insurance papers."

"I said it was insurance, darling. Insurance that I won't be left without anything once Tee-Bone is gone for good."

I should have questioned that "gone for good" thing, but was too dazzled by the diamonds to really notice.

"There must be a fortune there!" I exclaimed.

"More like a couple of fortunes," she giggled, and I saw her eyes sparkle in the dark. She grabbed me and kissed me, her tongue doing things to my mouth that set my blood on fire.

Curly glanced our way as we left the bar, and I saw her wink at him. I didn't care; she was going with me, and that's all that mattered.

Later, in a room off the highway at the Cactus Court Motel, she lay in my arms. I thought I'd died and gone to heaven, a trite phrase, but apt. She seemed satisfied, although a bit distracted. I just chalked that up to nervousness.

I finally rolled over and was just dozing off when she spoke. "You still have that gun you mentioned?"

"Sure, why?"

"I need another teeny little favor," she said, walking her hands up my leg.

"Sure, anything," I said. "What is it?" I said, pulling her closer, thinking about dinner.

She nipped at my ear with her teeth, ran her hands up my leg, her long nails scratching at my skin and whispered in my ear. "I need you to kill Tee-Bone."

"What?" I yelled, sitting upright.

"Shh! You idiot, someone will hear. These walls are as thin as paper."

"You can't be serious. I can't kill Tee-Bone. It wouldn't be right."

She shrugged. "It's really the only way you and I can ever be together. He's got me locked into a prison, and I'm not free to do anything. If I divorce him, the bar and everything that's his, will go to his son." She paused and shrugged again. "But, if he dies first ..."

"I thought you only wanted the insurance papers," I said. "And the diamonds?"

"I don't know why you're all riled up about it," she said, lighting a cigarette and blowing smoke in my face. "After all, it's only murder, my sweet."

Only murder? I was willing to do a lot to be with this woman, but not that.

Unless—unless I was sure I could get away with it.

"I'm sure you can get away with it," she said, as if reading my thoughts. "He works at the bar alone, after closing. Nobody else will be there if you go after two in the morning. You can get in and out without any problems since he leaves the back door open while he's working." She shook her head. "Stupid fool."

I blew out a breath. "OK, now, theoretically, how would this work?"

The next night, I dressed in a black tee shirt and jeans, feeling a bit foolish. I made sure that Aunt Gilda was sound asleep before I left. Billie had told me that Tee-Bone stayed at least another hour cleaning up, doing the books, restocking and so forth after closing.

I tripped over that damn tea cozy that was still in a wad in the kitchen floor and jabbed my ankle with one of my aunt's knitting needles, cursing under my breath. I stood stock still, then after a few moments, I decided I hadn't awakened her.

I blew out a breath, gently pulled the back door closed behind me, and was on my way.

The jukebox was still blaring when I pulled up alongside the Blue Orchid. I killed the headlights and listened for a minute. I heard muted strains of "Good Hearted Woman" by Waylon Jennings on the jukebox as I carefully closed the car door. I took a deep breath and crept up behind the joint. A thin light shone from the kitchen in back and I heard the clatter of beer bottles from the front. Good, he was working in the front, so I'd have the element of surprise.

I walked in and saw him standing behind the bar, his back to me. I took careful aim and fired. I heard his body thud to the floor, and I turned tail and ran. In the darkness, I looked into the big mirror behind the bar, got disoriented, turned around and ran for the front door. I slammed into it, setting off the alarm. I whirled around and ran through the back, tripping over Tee-Bone's body. I picked myself up, noticing that he had a beard, but didn't think much more about it.

I passed Sheriff Bailey as he raced to the scene going the other direction. I keep forgetting that Nameless is only about four blocks long and that the county offices were very close-by. It was a bit too close for comfort.

I was back home at Aunt Gilda's in less than fifteen minutes time and spent most of the night sitting up against the headboard of my bed, shivering. What had I done? I tried not to think about the dead body I'd stumbled over and kept my thoughts on Billie. There was something about the whole thing that bothered me but I couldn't put my finger on it. I finally dozed off into a fitful sleep, dreaming of bloody corpses with beards.

The next day, I pretended to be sick and stayed in bed. Aunt Gilda fussed over me for a bit then let me be. She had some kind of church thing to attend, some sort of quilting bee, I think, or maybe it was her scrapbooking club. Either way, she finally left the house.

I got up, took a long, hot shower, and called Billie. She seemed different over the phone, a bit hesitant, sullen. But finally she agreed to meet me at the diner. She said we had something to discuss, and I was eager to see her.

When I walked in, it was obvious that Billie had been crying. I rushed to her and took her in my arms and kissed her, but she pushed me away. She was acting strangely, so I tried to lighten the mood a bit.

"Now that Tee-Bone's out of the way, we can be together, maybe even get married," I said, smiling, but the joke fell flat.

She stared at me. "Marry you?" she said. "I have no intention of marrying you."

"But …" I started.

She seethed with anger. "You stupid idiot, you didn't kill Tee-Bone, you killed Curly! He and I were … very close. I can never forgive you for that."

"What? But I don't understand, you said that Tee-Bone would be working last night."

She shook her head. "He switched days off with the bartender. One night a week, Curly closes the place up for Tee-Bone. They changed the schedule at the last minute. Don't you even know what Tee-Bone looks like?"

"What?" I still didn't understand what she was saying.

"You heard me, you killed the wrong man! You stupid fool."

"We can still be together! We can make it right. I can make it right."

She just shook her head.

"But I fell in love with you! After all we've been through, I thought we …"

"We?" she sneered. "What part of there is no we do you not understand, cowboy? I can't believe you thought we'd get married," she laughed. "Don't you dare love me. Your love is a flame that will destroy you in the end. Don't you get it? I was playing you, using you."

"But, why?"

"To get what I want, of course."

"And what is that?" I asked. "You got the diamonds!"

"Don't be a dope! The diamonds are just chicken-feed. I want the Blue Orchid, of course. I want the bar."

So that's why she wanted Tee-Bone out of the way. Not so she could be with me—so she could have the bar. "I don't understand. Why would you want that stinking place?"

She laughed. "That stinking place, as you call it, makes about a million dollars a year in sales of Lone Star longnecks alone. Not to mention all the jukebox & cigarette-machine income. Tax-free, cash income."

"I had no idea," I mumbled.

"Curly McCloud and I were going to own it together after we got rid of Tee-Bone." She laughed. "He's such a stupid old fool, and this is no country for old men," she said. "Tee-Bone is so behind the times. He could be making twice as much money if he only had a lick of business sense."

"I can't believe that's why you wanted me to kill him," I said, incredulous. "For that stinking bar. I thought we had something good here."

"Yes, for the bar. And now, thanks to you, I'll have to come up with another plan to get rid of Tee-Bone. Anything we had went adios when you screwed up and killed the wrong man. Bumbling fool," she said, and got up to leave. She hesitated a moment and I thought she was changing her mind.

"At least you did get me the diamonds. So thanks for that." She turned to walk away, then stopped.

She reached into her bag and took out the packet. She removed one of the diamonds and put it on the table. "Consider this your payment."

I picked it up. "I don't want this; I want you!" I said, and was just about to hand it back to her.

Just then, the door flew open and Sheriff Bailey and his deputy crashed in like some damned TV lawmen, their weapons drawn and pointed straight at me.

I jumped up and whirled around, but there was no escape.

"Honey, what took you so long?" she cooed, slithering over to the sheriff and planting a huge kiss on his flabby lips and pressing her bosom into his chest.

He was momentarily distracted. "We had to make sure we got him, darlin'. You know that."

He turned to me. "You're under arrest for theft, and for murder," he said, and the deputy took me by one arm.

I shrugged him off, yanked my arm back and reached into the back of my jeans, pulling out my gun. Before any of them could react, I shot Billie where she stood.

She fell into the sheriff's arms. If I couldn't have her, I'd be damned if anybody else would, either.

As she fell, she dropped the packet and the diamonds spilled to the floor like so many stars.

"Farewell, my lovely," I whispered as I dropped my gun and put my hands up.

<hr>

She had played me for a fool, and I lost everything. I guess Aunt Gilda was right about her after all.

But you know what? It was worth it. Damned, but it was so worth it.

Billie Burkett was the last thing I thought about before they slammed the door to my jail cell. Now I sit on my bunk, whistling some sad little tune from some long-ago movie. Damned, I wish I could remember what it's called. Maybe it will come to me, as time goes by. One thing's for sure; I have time to think about it. Nothing but time.

What is it about a detective story that so entrances us? A detective is someone whose life is built on finding answers. Perhaps, we too, are forever in search of answers about ourselves?

Ms Kinnaman is the founder and editor of SW Montana Magazine, as well as host of an annual Writer's Conference to encourage and inspire other storytellers. Lynn wrote her first mysteries in grade school, testing them by reading to the neighborhood kids, and she's been writing and telling stories ever since.

Complete Deceit

by Lynn Kinnaman

The cat arched gracefully, its shadow falling against the brick wall, the only thing of interest within view from my office window. Winter's early evening darkness lay like a heavy blanket across the city. I poured another two fingers of bourbon and drank it in a single swallow. I could hear the hourly chime from a distant clock tower, my focus so complete I didn't notice the door to the outer office opened and didn't realize anyone stood there until she cleared her throat.

"Ahem. Excuse me, are you the investigator?"

She stood in the doorway, a plump woman with dark hair, streaked with gray, twisted into a bun atop her head. In her buttoned-down ankle-length dress and plaid overcoat, she appeared as out of place in this seedy part of town as a tea cozy in a billiard hall.

Still, clients being in short supply, I couldn't afford to be dismissive.

I took my feet off the desk, and stood.

"Peter Ellroy," I said. "At your service."

"Elsie Paddington," she said.

"Please, have a seat." I fought the urge to wipe the dust off the chair, grateful that she didn't seem to mind.

"What can I do for you?" I asked, resuming my seat.

"I need to find a murderer," she said matter-of-factly, as if placing an order for latte and a muffin.

Experience kept my reactions in check but my mind raced. She wasn't asking for a referral, was she?

"I see," I said, leaning back, forgetting for the moment that my chair had abandoned its grip on the reclining stop. As I moved past the tipping point, I saw the startled look in her eyes right before I crashed to the floor.

"Oh no!" she said, hastening to my side of the desk. "Are you all right?"

She extended her hand, but I had enough dignity left to refuse to let a woman old enough to be my mother haul me to my feet.

"I'm fine," I said, scrambling up and righting the chair. I covered my embarrassment by shifting into business mode. Setting a piece of paper in front of me, I prepared to take notes regarding Ms. Paddington's request. I was hoping she wasn't looking to hire a killer, it might create a moral dilemma. I wasn't doing well with those, lately.

"Now," I said, "can you tell me more about why you are looking for a murderer?"

Her expression reminded me of a teacher I had in grade school who tried, unsuccessfully, to be patient with her student's stupid questions. I'd seen that emotion too many times to count.

"For justice, of course," she said.

"Justice?"

She sighed, picking up her oversized purse and placing it on the desk. She scooted the shot glass and bottle to the side.

"Maybe this will help explain." She dug around, pulling out a newspaper clipping, which had become tangled in red string of some sort. A pair of knitting needles, a crochet hook, other odds and ends, and a ball of yarn popped out and rolled across the desk towards me. I made a grab for it, but it fell to the floor, continuing its journey across the uneven and filthy surface.

I retrieved it, trying to brush off the worst of the debris.

I handed her the yarn and she gave me the clipping. I scanned the headline.

Local Woman Killed in Attempted Robbery

The story gave the facts. A long-time resident died from a blow to the head in her home. The location was a suburb; a two-hour's drive from where we were. I looked at Ms. Paddington with narrowed eyes.

"What about the police? Why don't you leave this to them?"

She shook her head. "They aren't pursuing it. At least, not to my satisfaction."

"Why come to me? Surely there are people you could find who were closer, better acquainted with the area."

I looked longingly at my bottle.

I could quit any time. This wasn't the time. However I didn't feel comfortable pouring another shot in front of my new client.

"That's the point, really. I want someone with fresh eyes. Someone who has no preconceived ideas. I found you in the phone book."

It made sense in a weird way.

"Of course, you'll need to come to Travertine."

It made sense if I had nothing else to do.

Lucky for her I didn't, so I agreed.

I asked for my usual retainer, and she opened a bright orange wallet, counting out the bills. She handed them to me and I gave her a receipt. I must have been too cheap. Perhaps I should have doubled it, but money wasn't my strong suit. Curiosity motivated me.

The plan was that I'd drive out the following day, arriving in the afternoon, and she'd give me a tour, showing me the layout and the possible suspects.

She left, and as I went to lock up, I saw something under the chair. I bent down to retrieve it.

It was a business card. My business card. I didn't have any cards out. Had it been hiding in the general disarray of my office? In which case, why would it appear now?

Or had it fallen out of her purse?

If it had, that meant finding me was no accident, no serendipitous result of a phone book search.

Ms. Paddington had sought me out. The question was why?

I hastened on my way, urgency foremost in my mind. That harmless-looking woman had an agenda, and I couldn't wait to find out what it was.

———

Travertine looked like I'd pictured. A throwback small town, tucked away from the mainstream, somehow untouched by the slick citified environs I called home. With my early start, I had time to have a meal before letting Ms. Paddington know I'd arrived. I wanted to get a sense of the place before being influenced by the story I'd hear.

I took a seat at the lunch counter of the Deli-Belly Take-Out/Eat-In.

The server set napkin-wrapped silverware in front of me. "What can I getcha?"

"Is there a menu?"

She waved to the chalkboard behind her. "S'up there. Ya need a minute?"

I checked the board. The house special was a corned-beef sandwich with all the trimmings, and a look around the room reinforced my hunch that it would be a good choice. They looked fat and happy, just like the people eating them.

I ordered the special and coffee.

While I waited, I snagged a copy of the newspaper. I found a small write-up on the robbery murder on page five. According to the reporter, the police had pretty much hit a wall.

The server delivered my order. "You from the city?" she asked as she set the plate down.

"What gave me away?"

She shrugged. "Could tell a mile off." She squinted at me as if gauging my value. "What brings you to Travertine?"

I hesitated.

"You aren't a reporter, are you?"

Relieved, I denied the accusation and was rewarded with a smile. "Good," she said. "I don't like reporters."

I ate in silence, reading the news of promotions and an annual home show. When I finished, the woman returned with my bill.

"Do you know how I get here?" I asked, showing the address Ms. Paddington had given me.

She read the scrawl, then looked at me incredulously.

"Who gave you that?"

Her reaction surprised me. Something wasn't right, and I didn't need to draw on my investigative skills to see it.

"Why?" I asked. "Do you know where this is?"

She pressed her lips together.

I waited.

"Of course I do," she said, her voice low and flat. "I send flowers there on holidays every year." She tapped the paper. "That's the address of the Travertine Memorials Gardens."

At my blank look, she clarified.

"Travertine Memorial Gardens is the town cemetery."

<hr>

It wasn't that I didn't believe her.

I had to see for myself. I drove to the address, following the road up hill to the wrought iron gates. It was a cemetery. No doubt at all.

I parked on the road and shut the car off. Now what?

A small boy on a bicycle looked at me curiously and came over to the window.

"You lost, mister?"

The words, didn't your mother tell you not to talk to strangers? expired on my lips. Truth was, I felt very lost.

"How long has this cemetery been here?"

"About a hunnerd years," the boy said. "You have family here?"

I shook my head, but I had no idea, really. I'd grown up in a group home, with no clues about who my parents were or where they came from.

"My grandpa's buried there," the boy said. "You wanna see his grave?"

"Sure," I said, getting out of the car. I hadn't a plan on what to do, and walking the graveyard couldn't hurt.

"You ever hear of Elsie Paddington?" I asked the boy as we passed through the gates.

"Nah. Who is she?"

"Just a lady I met. She's the reason I'm here."

He looked up at me. "She pretty? You dating her?"

I smiled. "No. She came to me for help."

"What kind of help? What do you do?"

"I'm an investigator. She wanted me to look into something for her."

"Ahh," the boy said, nodding as if he understood. He stopped. "Here's my Grampy's grave. And Grammie's going right beside him."

We stood in front of an open hole, and a settled grave, marked by a block of etched granite, spanning both. A flowerpot displaying bright yellow blooms was tipped against the headstone and the boy set it straight.

"That's why I came today, to check on the flowers," the boy explained. "We have a bunch more for the memory service at our house tonight. I brought these here so Grampy wouldn't be left out."

"Your grandma died recently, then?" I asked without thinking too much about it, instead looking around to try to figure out why I'd been brought to this place.

"Yeah," the boy said. "Somebody tried to rob her. She got kilt."

I stared at the boy. "Your grandma was the woman killed in the robbery?"

"Yup," he said. "You heard of her? I think everyone knew Grammie. That's what momma says. You should come to our house for the service. There's gonna be food. Everyone's invited."

Clouds rumbled overhead.

"I gotta go," the boy said. "It's gonna rain. You stayin' or what?"

Good question.

"Is there a motel somewhere nearby?"

His face brightened. "My cousin Tony has a motorin."

"A what?"

"A motorin. Like what you said, a motel place. It's the Sleepyside Motorin."

Motor Inn, I deciphered.

I got the directions and we parted ways. The Sleepyside Motor Inn was easy to find and had rooms available. Travertine wasn't exactly on the must-see list of tourist attractions.

I checked in and found a phone book in the drawer. No listings for Elsie Paddington, but there were three Paddingtons listed. I called them all. No one knew an Elsie.

Still, Ms. Paddington had brought me here, paid for my investigative services and I needed to do something in return. But what?

I opened the newspaper I'd grabbed earlier and found an announcement for the memorial service. As the boy had said, it was open to the public. And refreshments would be served.

I'd been hired to find a murderer. I could start by meeting the victim's family.

The predicted rain came and went. At the appointed time I drove to the house, parking several blocks away in the only open spot I could find. Grammie had a lot of friends.

I walked to the home and stood in the front yard with other guests, listening to the conversations swirl around me.

"Hi! You came!"

I saw the boy from the cemetery. He took the hand of a woman and pulled her along with him to my side.

"Mom! This is my new friend I told you about."

His mom, her eyes red-rimmed, gave me a tired smile and held out her hand. "I'm Lorraine."

Lorraine. Icy fingers trailed lightly down my spine. It wasn't a real common name. I'd only known of one Lorraine.

I pushed that thought aside, but like a cobweb, pieces clung. I chose to ignore them.

"Peter," I said.

She had a nice, solid handshake. Confident and firm. "Joey said you knew my mother?"

"No," I said, unsure how to explain. "Do you know Elsie Paddington by any chance?"

Her answer was no, which didn't surprise me. I was beginning to wonder if Elsie even existed or if I'd hallucinated her.

"Please," Lorraine said, "come on in and meet the rest of the family."

I followed her inside and found myself greeted with hugs even though I didn't know anyone. At their insistence I took a seat on the sofa and someone offered tea. Before I could refuse, a cup of orange spice had been pushed into my hand.

"Cookie?" A small girl with huge brown eyes held out a plate of fragrant baked goods. Having learned my lesson, I took one without objection.

"We're celebrating my Grammie's life," she said solemnly. Then she grinned. "Grammie always liked a good party. Her favorite cookies are the chocolate sprinkle ones."

I munched the cookie and drank the tea, looking around the room. As my gaze drifted over to the corner, I froze. A basket of yarn was next to the fireplace, a round red ball of yard sitting on top. Two knitting needles poked out like antennae.

I finished my cookie, gulped the rest of the tea and stood up, crossing the room, ending up in front of the basket. One ball of yarn was just like another, wasn't it? It couldn't be the same yarn.

I wanted to touch it, but couldn't see how that would help me. I didn't see any foreign particles on it, stuff the yarn in my office had gathered rolling around on the floor. It could have been cleaned off, though.

It had to be a weird coincidence. Except this entire trip had been weird, if not coincidental. Underneath it all I had the strong feeling an unseen hand was orchestrating everything. Someone was moving the pieces about, but for what purpose?

I wandered down the hall, ostensibly searching for a bathroom, and saw the hallway was filled with photographs. I switched the hall lights on and started at one end, looking at the photos. I was working my back chronologically, and as I neared the early years, a chill came over me.

I stopped at a black and white photo. It showed a woman with a big smile, her arms around a boy and a girl, who were sitting in her lap. The girl appeared to be around four and the boy looked to be about two years of age.

The girl held a stuffed bear.

The boy held a red-heeled sock monkey by the tail.

How many kids grew up with a red-heeled sock monkey? How many besides the kid in this picture? And me?

I had the same sock monkey, or its twin, as the only remnant of a childhood of which I had no memory.

Coincidence? No way.

I was certain now. I'd been brought here for a purpose. The pieces of the puzzle fit. If my conclusions were correct, the reasons were obvious.

I'd just met my sister, the woman named Lorraine.

And the other woman, the one who'd been killed, had been my mother.

And Elsie, whoever she was, tracked me down because she wanted me to find the killer.

"That's my Grammie," Joey said, appearing beside me.

"And your mom?" I asked, pointing.

"Yes, and her lost brother."

"What happened to her brother?"

"He went with his daddy and they never came back."

"What was his name?"

"Joe. I was named after him."

Joe. It didn't feel familiar, but that meant nothing. I only knew what I'd been told. Found abandoned in the city, sent to a group home. Never claimed. Never adopted.

"Wasn't your Grampy Joe's daddy?"

"No," Joey said. "Grammie and him got married later."

Joey went back to the living room, while I studied the rest of the photos, thinking I could see a resemblance.

"I guess you've put it together," the voice at my side said. I recognized her instantly.

"Elsie!" I said. "Or should I call you something else? Like your real name?"

She blushed, looking abashed. "My name's Margaret. Renee was a friend of mine."

"My mother, you mean?"

"I think so," she nodded. "I think you are Lorraine's lost brother. Let's go somewhere and I'll tell you how this came about."

<hr>

We sat in a diner. I poked at the apple pie, overlaid by a slice of melting cheddar.

"Your pie okay?" Margaret said. She'd finished her slice of banana cream.

"Fine," I said.

Margaret explained how Renee had been told he and his father had died in a fiery car accident shortly after they'd left. She didn't know what had really happened. No one did. But Margaret couldn't let it go. A year ago, she'd begun to trace the family history, learning techniques on research she applied to Joe's disappearance.

She'd come up with some strong possibilities. Joe, or Peter, as he'd been named, was on her list of men to check out.

The robbery, and Renee's death, had made her willing to make a leap.

When she'd come to my office, seeing me face-to-face, I looked so much like Renee she had no doubt about the relationship.

"Why didn't you just tell me? Why the subterfuge?"

"Would you have believed me? Would you have come?"

I couldn't answer that.

"I know you have a, well, you've been dealing with uh …"

"I drink too much. I know. I do. But it's under control." I realized with surprise that I hadn't had a drop since I'd arrived in Travertine.

"You needed a purpose. Someone killed Renee, and I want them caught. I thought you could help."

I took a bite of the pie. It was better than I expected. I ate the rest while Margaret told me everything she knew and suspected about the robbery and murder.

We met at Renee's house in the morning. Margaret had a key and we ignored the flimsy yellow tape. The house had been tossed. Margaret showed me around and explained the police believed Renee fought back.

"They implied if she hadn't, if she'd just given up, she'd be alive today. They made it sound like it was her fault."

Margaret stayed out of the way while I searched the places I knew were usually overlooked. This woman was my flesh and blood. I felt as if I could step into her mind and think the way she did. Whether that was the case or whether I just tapped into my experience, I hit pay dirt within the hour.

"Eureka." I said, holding up a flash drive I'd found wrapped in plastic and buried in a flowerpot.

"I knew you'd find it," Margaret said. I turned to face her and saw she had a gun aimed at my heart. "Hand it over."

"I don't understand."

"Renee was my bookkeeper. She was a wee bit too efficient. She found some discrepancies that could ruin me. I knew she'd made a copy because she threatened me with it."

"Threatened you?" My mother was a blackmailer?

"She said I had a week to go to the authorities and come clean, then she'd do it for me."

"Why me? Why get me to do this?"

"I lied. Your mother was the one who had done the research. She had gotten close to finding you, but she ran out of time."

"Okay, I still don't get it. Why bring me into it?"

She smiled like a politician. "Just my own little joke. I hate Lorraine. Your mom left some money and she owned Lorraine's house. With you back in the picture, she'll have to share. With any luck, you two will squabble, hire lawyers, spend the money fighting and end up with nothing."

I could see she based her beliefs about other people's behavior on her own wicked ways. I couldn't care less about money or a house. If I was to be reunited with my family, it was worth twenty estates to me.

I didn't care to point out Renee's miscalculations. According to her, when the information on the flash drive became public, she'd spend time where she couldn't mess with anyone's life anyway.

Unless she shot me and got away with the evidence.

I did the first thing that occurred to me. I tossed the flash drive as hard as I could through the open door. It landed on the driveway, bouncing under her vehicle. We both followed it, arriving at the car at the same time. She lowered herself to the ground to try to reach the drive. I picked up the discarded gun and put it out of the way, then grabbed her ankles and jerked her back.

"Ow," she screamed, as she scraped along the concrete. Once she cleared the car, I pulled her arms behind her back and sat on her.

The neighbor stood gawking.

"Call the police!" I yelled.

He turned and ran into the house.

I could see the flash drive where it had landed. She hadn't been able to reach it.

We heard sirens approaching in only a few minutes, and the fight left Margaret. Suspecting a trick, I kept my grip tight until the cops arrived.

Once Margaret had been secured and removed, along with the incriminating evidence, I drove to my sister's house.

I used the time to try and figure out how to tell her that her long-lost brother was home.

At last.

It is with pleasure we include in this anthology a story featuring Little J, the streetwise street urchin, by Wenda Morrone. Some of you may have met Little J in "Gossamer Wings", published last year in the Untreed Reads anthology, "Moon Shot". Those familiar with Little J know that his age varies from story to story.

"Not sure why the stories come to me that way," says Ms Morrone. Regardless of how they arrive, her stories paint vivid pictures of life through the eyes of an unusually gifted small boy.

Little J's Sweet Potato Pie

by Wenda Morrone

"*You're six*, aren't you, Little J?" Gideon leaned against a trash can. "You should know about Thanksgiving."

Little J flamed. "You blind? I be nine. Course I knows. Street full of fools flying balloons big as elephants. Easy pickings."

"Seven, maximum," said Gideon. "There's more to Thanksgiving than the Macy's parade, it's our official feast day. Turkey—like chicken, only bigger, with substantially more breast meat."

"Forget Dolly Parton chicken and keep you eyes open, old man. You working."

Little J blew on his hands. November nights, wind prowled Harlem streets like a hungry animal, and he needed his fingers warm. Gideon might have fancy words, but he didn't have the moves any more, his hands shook, and Little J didn't have them down yet, though he practiced the livelong day. Only his speed kept them eating regular.

"There's a guy, ten o'clock," he said, "eyes for nothing but his lady."

"When will you learn? He's looking everywhere but her, checking if we appreciate his luck. He'd see if you blinked. Besides, that's no lady. Don't you recognize Vidalia?"

"Course I does. Just testing. Tell me more Thanksgiving shit."

"Cranberry sauce, mashed potatoes, stuffing, gravy, sweet potato pie …"

"You drunk and I ain't catch on? Nobody put potatoes in a pie."

"What you've missed, Little J." Gideon wagged his head. "Nothing could match my mamma's sweet potato pie. Taxi pulling up at The Meritage."

The Meritage was a restaurant on 96th and Lenox Avenue close to Central Park, small but fancy. People rushing to get there on time or pumped up with food and liquor when they left—either way, careless with their wallets. He and Gideon had had some fine meals from the dumpster, too.

"I has him."

"Wait for it, J."

Gideon's timing was still dead on. Little J danced with impatience as the passenger door opened, kept dancing until a black shoe and a navy trouser leg stretched to the sidewalk.

"Now," said Gideon.

Little J ran to catch his ma, ran for the subway, ran to scoop his baby sister out of traffic, ran for his life up Lenox Avenue. He had his head down ready to butt navy trousers in the belly when another man appeared out of nowhere. Too late. Little J rammed navy-trousers, navy-trousers slammed into the other man. Down they all went, kersplat!

Little J bobbed up, helped navy trousers to his feet, dusted off his soft brown coat and snow-white shirt, and tore off again. Around that corner and the next, slow to a walk, zigzagging at random until he found an empty block. He stopped in a doorway, turned his back to the wind and the street, stripped the cash from the wallet and thumbed it.

Two hundred dollars. A hundred at the front, a fifty at the back, in between only fives and tens—mostly singles. Hell. And navy-trousers took cabs and dressed rich? Liar.

Couldn't be helped. The hundred in one pocket, the fifty in a second, the rest folded small down his sock. Little J shined the wallet against his t-shirt and dropped it in the next trash can. Gideon's Rule Number Four. If some fool found it and used the credit cards, the cops wouldn't look past that fool for another thief.

Little J bought sandwiches and headed for the stoop where he and Gideon had slept for three nights now. Gideon awaited him, keeping his butt warm on a stack of newspapers.

"Well?" asked Gideon.

"Chicken shit." Little J handed over a ham-and-swiss. "Not even big enough for turkey shit. Fives, tens—mostly singles."

"You wouldn't hold out on me, would you?"

"Course I holding out on you. I ain't, you be drinking Thunderbird clear through to breakfast. No more than usual. Why?"

"I always wait and watch. See what we might be up against. Both men yelled Stop thief." Gideon's old eyes gave him a through-and-through. "Both."

"You see they second dude? Black suit? Skinny little tie? Yellow sunglasses? You think I messing with one of Mr. Sullivan's boys?"

Gideon kept looking. "I heard what they said to the police."

"They call cops about two hundred dollars?"

"They say they lost thousands. Each."

Little J thought about it. "Maybe navy-trousers carry more someplace. But why Mr. Sullivan's boy be lying? What they say about me?"

"They said it happened too fast, they didn't see."

"Ain't mean they ain't know. What else?"

Gideon's eyes went vague. Reading people was what he did best, but lately he couldn't keep himself together to talk for long. "You have my Thunderbird money?"

"Finish they sandwich."

Little J knew he should be tougher, but watching Gideon struggle to eat always undermined him. He forced himself to hold out until the old man worried down half his sandwich.

Little J handed him a five. "This all the Thunderbird you get." And a twenty. "Keep it this time. If somebody try to steal you shoes and I finds you been drinking you bribe money, you going barefoot."

It had happened too often for Gideon to protest. He shambled sheepishly away.

Little J set off for Sweet Vidalia's, a block down Lenox from The Meritage. The CLOSED sign showed. Little J scratched on the door anyway.

The shade hiked to one side to show a big brown eye. Vidalia cracked the door. "How'd you know I was in, brown sugar?"

"You date drop you off so close to home, it be the last one." He blew on his hands. "You axing me in? It cold enough out here to make a man's junk fall off."

Vidalia widened the door with a sigh. "If only it were that easy, Little J."

She had done the tits—had she ever, they overflowed her arms when she leaned on the counter—and had her Adam's apple shaved. Her cheeks were shiny smooth day and night. Now she was saving for the big surgery. She always paused and dropped her voice to say that: The Big Surgery.

She still wore tonight's wig, fat red curls heaped up. Gold dust glittered on her cheeks. Her yellow dress showed enough breast for a turkey. Lots of yellow dresses on her racks, too, and feathers. Vidalia was partial to both.

"Who you be tonight?"

Vidalia patted the red curls. "Lucille Ball."

Whoever that was. "I always partial to redheads."

"You must want something, Little J."

"Ain't me. Gideon." Little J took out a rubber band, working it between his fingers as Gideon had taught him, to make them flexible. "He on the mope. Talking about potatoes in pie."

Vidalia's eyes went as dreamy as Gideon's. "How that takes me back. My mama made the best sweet potato pie in south Georgia."

"You know about it, too? If it a real pie, why ain't I hear about it before?"

"It's only for Thanksgiving. You know, in November."

"This be November."

She nodded. "Thanksgiving is next Thursday."

"Already? Shit, I out of time. You make him a pie, Vidalia?" He added quickly, "I pay you."

"Do I look like a cook to you, Little J?"

"You a woman now, ain't you?"

Vidalia's laugh turned into a sigh. "I don't get many requests for cooking. I'll ask for Mama's recipe, but you'll need somebody else to bake it."

"Like who?" Vidalia knew everybody up and down Lenox Avenue.

Her eyes went dreamy again. "Try Barbados. He owns The Meritage? He does all his own baking."

Little J knew better than to trust a woman. "For true? Or you want to get into his pants?"

Vidalia's eyes turned stony. "You want Gideon to have sweet potato pie for Thanksgiving? Or not?"

Little J knew when to give up, too. "When you get me this recipe thing?"

Little J had learned from Gideon how to clean up decent. Sunday morning they went for a proper breakfast at the Brick Oven Cafe, so he could wash up in the men's room—face, ears, neck, arms—everything not hidden by a t-shirt. After breakfast he scrubbed again before he put on a new shirt. He even smelled different afterward. He had to hang around the alley side of The Meritage and wait—without picking up dirt—because it was Sunday, and they always did a bang-up business. Called it brunch and charged according.

It was one-thirty before kitchen boys commenced filing out the back, stripping off aprons so he knew they'd be gone a while. He caught the back door on the swing and eased inside.

He was in an unlighted room. Nothing fancy—shelves floor to ceiling, a rough plank floor, rows of barrels. Only a narrow path to the lighted doorway beyond. He tiptoed there and peered around the edge.

Good thing he had scrubbed. This room gleamed: red tile floor, stainless steel stoves and counters and fridges, shiny pots hanging. A wood-topped table with knives along the back. A big dude stood there, his white jacket cleaner than a television doctor's. Only his hat, a bill cap, looked the worse for wear. Well, and his face. He looked like a man who never expected a good thing again. Which didn't make sense, after Meritage's fine morning. This had to be Barbados.

Little J sussed him out—a big man with more face than he needed—bunchy cheeks, big nose and chin. Vidalia couldn't want him for his looks.

He pushed up against the table behind the knives and craned to see over them. "You be Barbados? On account of, you ain't look Latin."

The man's gaze came from a long way away, like a dead man's. "Barbadian," he said. "Janos Barbadian. I'm Armenian."

"You talk like a American."

"One can be both. How did you get in my kitchen?"

Not who are you. Not get out. Too far gone to care. "Come in the back way." Little J jerked his chin. "I has business with you. Only Vidalia say you Barbados."

"Vidalia?"

"She own Sweet Vidalia's, up on Lenox?" Little J sketched her with his hands, especially the tits. Barbados' eyes came back to life so Little J could see there was a lot of man inside after all. Somewhere. "Maybe Barbados a pet name?"

Barbados stirred. "You're a friend of Vidalia's? What does she want?"

Like he didn't have an idea. Like that wasn't why he was wriggling.

"Not her," said Little J. "Me."

He slid an envelope from under his t-shirt and eased out the paper. Just one page. He had to trust Vidalia that it was the recipe—he could do numbers fine, but words always seemed to dance around on him. He watched Barbados read it.

Barbados slapped it. "Vidalia wants me to bake potatoes in a pie? Does she know nothing about The Meritage? I am unique. I blend Middle Eastern and Mediterranean and French. This … this…" He slapped it again.

"They sounds foreign," said Little J. "This be a American pie."

"That, certainly. Thank Vidalia for the honor, but no."

Little J stood his ground. "This a fine place, Barbados. The pie need to be fine, too. It for a old man who on the mope. Only they ain't much time. I needs it Thursday." Something about Barbados' expression made him wary. He added, "Ain't a favor, I pay you. "Now he saw what was wrong: Barbados looked like a dead man again. "Oh, if you'll pay. Three thousand dollars. That's my price."

The number was too unreal to have anything to do with pie. Little J only needed a second to make the leap.

"That your weekly vig to Mr. Sullivan? His boy be carrying it last Friday?"

Barbados' face went blank. "If I knew what you were talking about…"

"Everybody pay Mr. Sullivan," Little J said impatiently. "He axing to get paid all over again? On account of his boy getting forked?"

Barbados took a knife and examined the edge as if he saw dirt. Little J backed a step. Barbados raised the knife and lowered it. It looked easy, but the knife jammed into the wood table and hung there shivering.

"By Wednesday," Barbados said to the knife. "Since Thursday is Thanksgiving and The Meritage will be closed. My regular payment on Friday as usual."

"Hot business like this," said Little J, "bank hand you three thousand and shake you hand."

"A new hot business like this, little friend of Vidalia's, skates from bill to bill. Even without Mr. Sullivan's fee. I can't make both payments. Next week I'll have all day everyday to make this..." He snapped his fingers at Vidalia's mama's recipe.

"Ain't help. My man need his pie on Thanksgiving."

Barbados smiled a smile with no smile in it. "Then find my money. Do that, and I'll make you Thanksgiving dinner to go with your pie."

Barbados giving up didn't mean Little J had to. "What time Wednesday?"

Barbados squinted like he thought Little J was bluffing. He gave a what-the-hell shrug. "Walter comes at six o'clock."

Little J wanted to crouch. He stopped himself. "You say Walter?"

"You know him?"

"Everybody know Walter. No wonder you scared. He be here six o'clock Wednesday? Expect me before then with you money."

"Expect who, exactly?"

Little J stuck out his chest. "Somebody tell you Little J be here, that be me."

<hr>

"Our snatch last Friday," Little J said to Gideon. "Tell me about the dude in the cab. Wore navy trousers."

They sat in the thin afternoon sunshine on a sidewalk bench. Benches belonged to whoever got there first. Little J worked his rubber band. Gideon looked to be dozing, but it was early, this should be his prime time. Not hungry, not drunk.

He didn't open his eyes. "Why? We've scored twice since then."

"I has a job getting they Friday money back. Needs to know where to look."

Gideon opened an eye to look down at him. Little J concentrated on the rubber band.

"You're not good enough yet to go on your own," Gideon said.

"I knows that. I ain't even snitch you bribe money without I wake you, even when you drunk. How I going to bounce somebody by myself?"

"Then how can you get the money back?"

Why did people—even Gideon—so often get things backward?

"How can I tell before I knows where it be? If Mr. Sullivan have it, the dude be dead already. So navy-trousers still have it. Tell me about him."

Gideon said, "If I'd seen his shoes in time, I'd have stopped you. His coat was fine. Shirt, suit, tie. But his shoes were cheap and he didn't take care of them."

Now that Gideon mentioned them, Little J could picture them, too. "Dusty, wasn't they?"

"And the heels were worn." Gideon said as one who knew, "He's in our line of work, J."

Little J should have spotted it himself, instead of wasting time being disgusted at his skinny take. "He working The Meritage, same as us?"

"I don't mean he works the street or works with his hands. I don't know what he does. But he's working."

Little J thought back. "His money. He have big bills front and back, little ones in between."

"Ah. He has to flash a thick wad to convince people to give him a thick wad of their own to invest."

"He see a chance to fork Mr. Sullivan's boy while I forking him, and he take it. If he local, he know better. So he ain't. Must of gone to The Meritage to meet a mark. I starts there."

Gideon closed his eyes again. "I don't even want to think how you're going to do that."

"Simple. Barbados a friend of mine."

"Really. You met over his dumpster?"

Little J pretended he hadn't heard.

Later that afternoon he rang stepped inside Sweet Vidalia's. Vidalia was helping two women—trannies like her, though not so flossy—poke through her dress racks. She switched her gaze from them to him and back.

"Come back later, Little J. I'm working."

"Me, too. Ain't got no later."

She gave him the same you're-bluffing look Barbados had. She shrugged like him, too, only she was nicer to watch. "Wait in my office. Don't touch anything."

Fine with him. He took the papers out from under his shirt—two sheets this time—put them on Vidalia's desk, and waited. Waited some more.

Finally Vidalia appeared in the doorway, hands on hips. "Well?"

"Who you today, Vidalia?"

She smoothed brown hair that flipped up at the ends. "Diana Ross of the Supremes. Well?"

Little J said handsomely, "Say this, Vidalia. Maybe you pretending to be a woman, but they always mighty fine women."

"What do you want, Little J?"

He popped it right out. "Barbados in the shit. If I saves his ass, he make Gideon's sweet potato pie."

She plumped down on her office chair. So maybe her thing for Barbados was real. It better be.

"What kind of trouble?"

"You know about they mix-up in front of The Meritage last Friday? Mr. Sullivan's boy and another dude?"

"I'm deeply sorry for the thieves. But they should have known better."

"Only there wasn't no thieves. I forks the dude. He forks Mr. Sullivan's boy."

Vidalia looked around her tiny office and out to her shop and the front door as if checking for a secret camera or a bug. Looked at him as if he was another kind of bug. A cockroach.

"I think I don't know you any more, Little J."

"You got PMS, Vidalia? This ain't no time to throw a mood. Mr. Sullivan's boy carrying Barbados' vig, and they telling him to pay it again by Wednesday. Only he can't."

Her eyes embiggened. "What will he do?"

Little J stuck out his chest. "Ain't you worry, I getting it back. Only I needs you help. We has to find the dude who stole Mr. Sullivan's money."

"We can trust Mr. Sullivan for that, Little J."

"If he from around here. But he ain't, on account of if he from around here, he know better. Also he be dead. So he from away. We has to make him come back."

Vidalia picked up a clump of papers and fanned herself. "I'm listening."

"Gideon say he a hustler. Why he come to The Meritage? To meet a mark. You know everybody on the street." Little J held up the two sheets. "These be Friday's reservations. Barbados make me a copy. Take a look. Who be the mark?"

It only took a glance. She gave an unladylike snort. "Freddy MacReady. If ever a man deserved to be fleeced..."

Simple as that? "You knows him?"

"You know him, too, brown sugar. Ready Freddy the fixer. He'll sell you a house and help you make it ready."

"Take a million to fix and he know the fixers?"

"Something like that."

"Gold tooth? Bitty mustache?"

"That's the man. Maybe your friend wants to buy a house."

Little J shook his head firmly. "Gideon ain't be wrong about him."

"Then we're done?"

He shook his head No. "How I hook Ready Freddy? Has to be you. You tells him you tired of waiting to have..." He paused and lowered his voice the way she always did. "your Big Surgery. You wants to invest you savings, pick the money up quick. He know anybody with a inside track? He sure to have you meet our man."

She fanned herself so hard her wig lifted. "And then?"

"You sets up a meet at The Meritage for lunch next Wednesday. I gets the money from him and gives it to Barbados. Barbados give it to Walter. Gideon get his sweet potato pie."

He didn't add, And Barbados would see her as a heroine. She could picture that part for herself.

"And if this man can't come up with the money?" she asked. "Or won't?"

"I has two other options. Third option, you loans Barbados the money from you surgery savings. But don't worry, we ain't need that. The second option be sure-fire."

"I think I should know what it is."

Little J patted her arm. "I ain't want to worry you, Vidalia."

She stopped fanning and gave him a look as if she was trying to reach right inside his head. "How old are you, Little J?"

Why did age matter to people? He flared. "We be personal now? When you getting they balls cut off?"

She shook her head. It kept on shaking, like a bobblehead. "Maybe not as soon as I planned. I'll call Freddy."

<hr>

Gideon told them what to expect from navy-trousers and coached Vidalia on how to handle him. Little J was damn proud. Time people saw he was more than an old man who guzzled Thunderbird every night until he fell asleep in the shadows.

Vidalia wavered from nervous to excited and back again until her cab pulled up to The Meritage—a cab, to take her a block. But when Freddy MacReady helped her out and practically kissed her hand, she commenced behaving like Vidalia again. She wore a platinum wig, not as fussy as usual. Classier.

By the time Black-tie settled her and Freddy at the table near the kitchen that Barbados had arranged, Little J was in position, behind the swing door between kitchen and dining room. Waiters and the black-tie man in charge of the dining room sighed as they squeezed past him, but Barbados had given him the okay. After he tripped one, they behaved.

Little J knew the outside of The Meritage, and he had been in the pantry and the kitchen. Wednesday was his first sight of the dining room. No wonder people liked it. One wall was all wine bottles, and for sure none was Thunderbird. Cloth covered every table down to the floor. Bunches of flowers, too, and forks and knives that looked about too heavy to lift.

Ten minutes, twenty minutes, half an hour late. Which wasn't bad—the emptier the restaurant was when the dude arrived, the better. Just the same, Little J was on the fidget when he finally breezed in, wearing the same navy suit. He had a weary smile, like all the money he'd made that morning had worn him out. Hair a little thin. Everything about him said money except his shoes. Still dusty.

Little J couldn't hear, but he didn't need to. MacReady with a wide smile, gold tooth showing, hands wide, too, waving to tell Vidalia navy-trousers was the real deal and to assure him she was, too. Navy-trousers leaned back shaking his head a little, not so eager, so Vidalia would have to make the running.

From behind the door, Little J said Huh. Like Vidalia didn't know all about who ran who. She gave Freddy a Who-is-this-shit? look and stood up to leave. Navy-trousers leaned forward damn quick. From then on she had him.

Little J watched the back-and-forth like a teevee. Vidalia wanting to know what he could do for her. Him drawing half a dozen pictures on the air, each one fancier than the last. Vidalia asking details. Him shrugging to say it depended on how much she put into it. Exactly as Gideon had described.

One more step.

Vidalia opened her big shiny purse and took out an envelope. Navy-trousers put out a hand. Her fingers beckoned: show me your money. He shrugged again—he was big on shrugging—and slid a hand inside his jacket.

Little J's cue. He pushed the door open.

The table was right there, but the walk seemed to take minutes. He kept thinking about how clean he was. About his brand-new t-shirt and jeans. The damn pie was getting expensive.

When he swung a chair around and sat, MacReady tried to shoo him.

Vidalia said, "I asked him to come. Little J, you know Freddy. This is Charley Farino."

Farino nodded without a smidge of recognition or interest.

"Farino ain't the name on your credit cards," Little J said like he knew for sure. "Ones in the wallet I fork."

Farino stared. "You're the kid who stole my wallet? You admit it?"

"Admitting something else, too. I see you fork Mr. Sullivan's boy."

Little J stayed fixed on Farino, but he heard MacReady's chair scrape back. Vidalia said, "Sit, Freddy." The chair scraped forward again.

Farino's face pulled clear back to the skull. He had to strain to switch back to Vidalia, but his voice sounded perfectly easy. "This lunch isn't working out. Maybe some other time."

Little J wished he could say sit like Vidalia. Instead he said, "I ain't see how much Mr. Sullivan's boy Walter carrying, but three thousand belong to a friend of mine. I only axing for that. The rest be yours."

Farino didn't look impressed.

Little J had hoped mentioning Mr. Sullivan a couple of times would be enough, but even MacReady muttering a breathless Walter didn't faze Farino. Little J had trouble picturing a world where a man didn't know Mr. Sullivan. Would his second option even work?

"If I don't give you the money, kid, what will you do?" Farino asked. "Call the police? Admit you stole my wallet?"

Little J sighed. "Too bad for you, I has a second option. I has pictures of you. Took them from behind that door." He jerked his chin toward the kitchen. "I offer them to Mr. Sullivan, he be happy to buy them. He'll want to talk to Mr. MacReady, here, get you phone number..."

MacReady scraped his chair back again. Little J said, "Mr. MacReady, tell Mr. Farino about Walter."

MacReady shook his head so vigorously, maybe it was scarier than anything he could say. But you never knew.

"I wants to tell Mr. Sullivan how helpful you be," Little J said to get him started. "Ain't Walter the one, he like hands?"

MacReady tried to swallow. He smiled like he'd rather throw up. Farino looked thoughtful.

"Walter's an enforcer," MacReady said. Finally. "He hurts people. Their hands. They say he likes it. Takes his time. It ... you don't use them again."

Farino looked down at his hands as if he'd just remembered how much he liked them.

"That if you lucky," Little J added. "If you ain't? Mr. Sullivan have a parking garage where he take people." Vidalia and MacReady said Hush and Don't, but Little J kept talking. "I ain't say you ain't come out again, but you ain't know you coming out. See what I mean?"

Farino's forehead beaded up with sweat. About time. He gave Little J an honest look only a fool would trust. "I don't have that much on me."

"I be sure to explain that to Mr. Sullivan. He probably understand."

Farino bared his teeth. "You're a bad-luck brat if ever I saw one." He fumbled inside his jacket and took out bills.

"Count them out," Little J said.

Thirty hundreds. When Little J stretched out a hand, Farino covered the money with his own.

"How do I know you won't tell this Mr. Sullivan anyway?"

"You ain't. Only this way you has a head start."

He didn't have to say that twice before Farino was up and gone. Not waiting for a cab, trotting toward Central Park with an arm raised for cabbies to spot him.

Vidalia and MacReady stared at Little J, not talking, not moving.

"Told you we ain't need the third option, Vidalia," he said. "That white hair be fine. Whose that be?"

She heaved in an awesome breath before she moistened her lips and whispered, "Carol Channing."

Would she ever do somebody he knew? "Wear that on Thanksgiving? When we has the sweet potato pie?"

"Will you really tell Mr. Sullivan?" she asked faintly.

"Think he listen to a kid?"

"So you didn't take pictures, either."

"Where I get money for a camera?" Little J scuffled the bills together into a stack. It felt good. One day he'd have a stack all his own. "You excuse me, I has business with Barbados."

<hr>

When Little J and Gideon rapped on The Meritage's alley door Thanksgiving afternoon, it was already a good day. The fools at the balloon parade were as careless with their wallets as drunks. He and Gideon were set for a week.

Barbados had set up a table in the middle of the dining room—tablecloth, flowers, silver—just like for paying customers. Vidalia wore the Carol Channing hair.

Barbados did the dinner up fine, too: a Vidalia-breasted turkey. Red sauce spiky as good salsa, but sweeter. Potatoes and gravy, stuffing and more gravy. How could a pie beat Barbados' gravy? They might as well give up and call it Barbados instead.

Finally Barbados said, "The piéce de resistance," and set down a pie.

Little J couldn't let that pass. "I ain't bargain for no piéce, Barbados, I ax for sweet potato pie."

Vidalia nudged him and whispered, "That's what it is, brown sugar."

He couldn't see potatoes. The pie was gold, almost orange, smooth and thick. At the first stab of his fork, the crust crumbled. He was embarrassed for Barbados. But Vidalia said, "Flakier than my mama's," so crumbs must be good.

His first bite went down so smooth he thought he'd missed something. He took a second bite to be sure, and next thing he knew his plate was empty. The second slice, he decided there was something deep to it he needed more of, but what?

Gideon put his head to one side and said, "Bourbon. Why didn't my mama think of that?"

The old man held out his plate and ate his second piece, too, down to the crumbs. That ought to hold him.

Our last story, appropriately titled, "The Last Dinner", serves up a tasty dish of murder, seasoned with a dark sense of humor, and served on a bed of fresh revenge.

John Haas' fiction has appeared recently in the anthologies, "100 Doors to Madness", "Paranormal Horror 2", and "Grimm & Grimmer Volume 3". The story Mr. Haas has penned for us is perhaps more grounded in reality than those, but no less macabre for it.

The Last Dinner

by John Haas

Richard Lassiter took in the luxurious table settings in the spacious dining room. Fine china, polished silver, white linen table-cloth with matching napkins, and all of it for chili. He appreciated the irony.

For the last two decades Richard had been Sam Carter's bodyguard and all-around man Friday. The bodyguard duties were light—animal activists demanding to know how many cows Sam had murdered, or enthusiastic foodie fans wanting his autograph—but he kept an eye on those close to Sam too. It was an occupational hazard not to trust anyone but he could swear he caught hungry looks, like young lions waiting for the father of the pride to grow weak.

Every June Sam invited the executives of Carter's Chili—mostly family—to the mansion for a long weekend. The first night was for trying new recipes, and while Sam concerned himself with chili, the others spent their time impressing Sam with their love and loyalty. No one wanted to be forgotten when it came time for the will, especially now.

Six months ago Sam had been as healthy as any other forty-five year old. Then the memory problems came, along with muscle spasms, occasional confusion, disorientation. Within two months Sam was confined to a wheelchair, no longer having the coordination to walk. Creutzfeldt-Jakob Disease—a horrible, wasting violation that attacked the brain and spinal cord, the human equivalent of mad cow disease. Sam's case, the most rare kind, was believed to be contracted through eating contaminated meat. Sam's executives had made sure that fact stayed away from the media. The rumors alone would sink the company.

The guests drifted into the dining room, each of them early for the eight o'clock dinner. Richard greeted them as they entered—Sandra, Sam's second wife; Brent Lewis, the business partner; Sam's brother Daniel, sister Loren and her husband Oskar. All of them involved in the business one way or another, except for the sister whose pride was too strong to work for her little brother—but not so strong she wouldn't marry his marketing executive. No kids this weekend. In the past the mansion had been open to everyone's children too. Sam loved them dearly, but he couldn't face them this time, not even his own sons.

Guests in place, Richard exited the dining room and returned pushing the wheelchair. Sam slouched in the seat, muscles jumping under his loose shirt. He frowned at the group as if they were strangers before a smile came to his face. The expression was a mockery of the vibrant man they had known, but Sam still lived in those eyes. "Thank you all for coming" he said, with heavy, slurred speech.

Richard took his place behind Sam; this meal was not for him. He observed his employer and friend, heeding Sam's order on staying alert for the more extreme symptoms of CJD: Dementia. Personality changes. Hallucinations.

Richard had urged him to cancel this year's gathering, but Sam wouldn't hear it. Sam Carter did things his own way, from business to personal dealings, and that had made him wildly successful. Behind each decision lurked a well thought out reason, no matter how bizarre or incomprehensible it might seem.

"One last dinner," Sam said.

"Ah, don't talk that way, Sam," Brent said in his sonorous voice. "We'll be doing this again next June, and you'll be sitting right there."

Sam was quiet a moment. "Maybe," he allowed. "Maybe. People with CJD sometimes survive as much as two years."

Was that a worried look on Daniels face, covered in a blink? The brother fidgeted in his seat. "Good," he stammered. "That's good, Sam. By then there might be a cure."

"Hah!" Sam's brief cackle was unlike him. He paused, calming himself. "No, Danny. No cure. No hope."

Daniel watched his brother a moment before dropping his gaze.

Heavy silence pressed in on them until Loren rushed to fill it with her usual mindless chatter and self-promotion. She started with talk about their parents and time growing-up; how she had been a second mom to her younger brothers.

"Yep," Daniel said, "she ordered us around whenever Mom was too busy,"

Sam laughed.

A storm cloud crossed Loren's face and her mouth snapped shut. Daniel kept the conversation rolling, adding how much he idolized his big brother, and how grateful he was to be in charge of the financials at Carter's Chili. Loren's husband, Oskar, did his part, talking about the direction Carter's Chili would take in the coming years. Sandra, Sam's wife and HR director, rested her hand on Sam's, an expression of deep affection on her face.

The door to the kitchen opened and rich aromas of chili powder, beef and cumin filled the dining room. Servers brought bowls of steaming chili and deposited them in front of each person. Corn bread, shredded cheese and hot sauce were placed in the center of the table.

The group turned to Sam. Usually he had a few words to say on the chili but this time he was asleep in his seat, spoon beside his full bowl. After glances at each other they started eating. Sam came in and out of dozing as they ate until the very end when every bite was finished and they were exclaiming how great this latest recipe was.

"My apologies," he explained. "Tired so often now."

Sam made a gesture and Richard stepped forward, grabbing the back handles of the wheelchair. He turned Sam and the chair toward the door.

"Bed for me," Sam said as they exited. "Stay. Eat."

Daniel closed his laptop and peered out the window into the deep darkness. Rain had arrived in a steady beating drone sometime during dinner.

After the perfect day of heat and sun it seemed like a gloomy omen, matching Daniel's mood.

His fingers drummed against the computer, his mind digesting the high priority e-mail he had read. It was official: they were four months away from the financial audit at Carter's Chili. Four months until they discovered Daniel's creative accounting. Sam wouldn't go easy just because Daniel was his brother. When the truth came out Daniel would be headed to prison. Four months to fix it. Inheritance money would allow him to replace the money, or get the hell out of the country and disappear.

He'd observed Sam at dinner, weighing all the symptoms: muscle spasms; slurred speech; instances of confusion, like Sam didn't know where he was. And Daniel wasn't sure who Sam thought he was fooling with that wig, but the rug on his brother's head was pretty obvious—an effort to cover ugly surgical scars, he guessed. Of course, no one here was going to point out the emperor's new clothes. The end result of Daniel's symptom tally was that Sam was declining fast; but was it fast enough? He'd done his research on the disease and knew two years was a pipe dream. Six months was possible though, and that would spell disaster.

He truly did love his brother, but Sam needed to die, and he needed to die soon.

***

"I hate chili," Oskar complained from the en-suite bathroom as he attempted to brush the taste out of his mouth.

Loren removed her panty-hose on the bed. "You did well, I wouldn't have guessed you were hating it."

"Hmph, I pretended each spoonful was a million dollars," he said around the toothpaste.

"We'll have our bite soon enough."

"No. If he died this minute it wouldn't be soon enough. I hate chili on these weekends. I hate chili when I have to visit the restaurants. I hate it when we test the canned crap at work."

"Inevitable part of the job," she said.

Twenty years ago he had joined the fledgling restaurant as its entire marketing department and been instrumental in expanding from a Texas-based fast-food chain to the international phenomenon Carter's Chili had become. Recently they had started canning and selling the chili in the supermarket. That idea, worth millions, had been his ten years ago.

Loren tossed him a roll of antacids.

"Thanks," he sighed. "This is the only thing I eat more of than chili." Oskar crossed the room and plopped next to Loren. "Are you sure he'll be dead soon? I can't do two more years. I can't. Maybe we should ... you know."

"Can't say it?"

Oskar stared at her. It was one thing to hate your job and your product, it was quite another to kill your employer, but that's what they had planned before this illness came along. An accident, a hit-and-run—

"He'll be dead soon. One way or another," she said.

The antacid in his mouth tasted like chalk—an improvement. He grabbed a magazine, headed for the bathroom. "Chili. The meal that keeps on giving."

———————

Loren closed the door to the bedroom as she left. Having shared a home with Oskar for more than ten years she knew she didn't want to experience the aftermath of chili.

The familiar fury seized her as she wandered the halls of the mansion. Her split-level bungalow was nice and new and modern but next to Sam's home, it was a crap-shack.

Her brother brought them here to gloat, revenge against the bossy older sister who had made him toe the line growing-up. No. No, his success was revenge, these weekends were for rubbing salt in the wound.

She'd been the big sister, the one who had gone to university, gotten good marks and been the good girl. Sam had bummed around Europe for more than a year after school, then came back and started a business that was doomed to failure. But it hadn't failed. She should have been the success story, instead she was only Sam Carter's sister.

When Sam was in the ground and the inheritance was in her hand she could stop playing the loving sister. The end was in sight but that only made each minute more agonizing than the last.

———————

Sandra lay naked under the sheets of Brent's bed as the rain beat against the window.

"Miserable night," he said from across the room.

"Good reason to stay inside."

"Oh, did I need another one?"

Sandra pulled back the sheets and patted the mattress beside her. Brent came over and crawled back into bed. "Something wrong?" she asked.

He hesitated. "He looked like hell tonight, didn't he?"

"Yes, he did."

The thought of his oldest friend dying in this house should have filled him with sadness, but all Brent could think of was how much easier it would be once Sam was gone.

"Why Brent, are you contemplating the demise of my dear husband? I am shocked."

"Dear husband?" Brent snickered. "Come here, I'll give you something that will shock you."

Later they resumed their conversation.

"Five months now he's been sliding downhill," Brent said.

"Can't be much longer, my love. Then it will all be ours."

"All of it?" Brent raised one eyebrow. It was what he wanted, what he dreamed of, hoped for. Controlling interest in Carter's Chili, but more than that, it meant Sandy would be all his.

"Of course," she agreed, slipping into his arms. "At the funeral you'll stand next to me, arm around my shoulders, comforting me. I'll be quite distraught, inconsolable really. The will comes next and we'll see how much he's left me. It will only be natural that we spend time together as you help me adjust. Then, after an appropriate amount of mourning, we bring our we-never-expected-this-to-happen relationship public."

"You've thought of every angle."

"I have."

"Have you considered what to do if he hangs on too long."

She nodded. "I have a couple of ideas on that. Stairs are not a friend to a man in a wheelchair."

Brent traced a line along the side of her body as she spoke.

Sandra let herself into the dim hallway. She peered behind her at the shadowed, snoring lump under the sheets. Brent was a dear, and a lot of fun in bed, but after she had Sam's money and business to herself she wouldn't need a man again except for the obvious reason, and Brent could still fill that need if he liked. She would need him on board until she was established as the new boss, but marriage? Never again. As it was, she felt like some animal with a paw caught in the steel trap jaws, ready to gnaw it off to escape. Well, escape was close, she could smell it. And like the aroma of something you cannot quite have, it was maddening.

Like Brent said, she had thought of every angle. The only problem was it was taking too damn long.

In the end, Sam's death took less than three months.

Richard led the way to the entertainment room. Colson Manchester, Sam's lawyer, followed close behind, black leather briefcase hanging by his side. He was a distinguished, older gentleman who reminded Richard of a country lawyer. Once inside the room, the lawyer set about his tasks, turning the entertainment system on, and inserting a DVD.

"A video?" Richard asked.

The lawyer nodded and continued while Richard sank into one of the chocolate brown leather couches. It was a testament to Sam's theatrical flair that they were all called here today for the reading of his will. What Sam wanted he got, even in death.

Richard contemplated the familiar room. Today would be his last day as a resident of the house. After the reading of the will he would go upstairs, collect his things and be gone for good. Sandra Carter had informed him his services would no longer be required and with Sam gone he was happy to leave.

As if called by his thoughts, Sandra bustled into the room, Brent Lewis close enough to be her shadow. Brent headed for the bar in the corner to pour himself a drink. On the way back he collided with the corner of the pool table and sloshed some onto the carpet. The two took places on the next couch over, not even acknowledging Richard's presence. Sandra, dressed in black, pressed her ever present tissue to her eyes though Richard saw no sign of actual tears. Within minutes Daniel, Loren and Oskar arrived, having let themselves in as they never would have a week ago. And just like that, the house was no longer Sam's.

Manchester looked around at the group. "Well, to make this even more interesting," he started in his slow drawl. "Sam gave me a video to play with explicit instruction that no one, not even myself, was to view it before today."

Richard laughed then gave an apologetic wave as everyone turned toward him. It certainly was like Sam to be so dramatic. He imagined there would be several instances of Sam telling people what they needed to hear before handing out inheritances.

"I have the paper will, all legal and witnessed, but the video has some extras, as Sam put it." Manchester stepped back, pointing the remote.

Sam's face popped up on the television. A somewhat healthier Sam, sick, but still a good month away from the wheelchair.

"Hello everyone," Sam said in slightly slurred speech. "Thank-you for coming." He chuckled, then took a drink from the water glass next to him. "Okay, so I can hear you all now: Why the hell are we here? Well, you know why. You all want to see how much." He rubbed his fingers and thumb together, then held up a hand. "I know, I know, not what you mean. You want to know why you're here, watching a video, instead of doing this the regular way, the proper way, as my sister might say."

Loren ignored the glances sent her way, sitting ramrod straight and staring at the television.

Sam leaned forward and gazed into the camera. "We're doing it this way because I want to, because I'm rich, and because I have some things to say. Now, Manchester has my encouragement to pause this any time you people get unruly."

Sam's muscles twitched and he observed the spasm, curiosity on his face, then looked back to the camera with a shrug. "First things first. There will be a murder soon."

The room plunged into complete silence. On screen, Sam waited for his revelation to sink in.

"Murder?" Manchester asked, bewildered. "Who's murder?"

"His own," Richard guessed. He examined the others, looking for some sign of guilt, some tell. Who would risk everything to speed Sam's death by a couple of months? Nothing in anyone's reaction made them seem more guilty than another. And if Sam had seen it coming, why hadn't he told Richard?

The lawyer paused the video. "I think I should call the police."

Was it possible for the room to get more quiet? Richard stood and crossed the room, positioning himself in front of the door. "Not yet, Mr. Manchester. I think we need to hear more of what Sam has to say."

Violent crime was outside of the lawyer's field of expertise and Richard could see the man's brain working. What did he really have to call the police with? A suggestion of murder from a dead man. He wouldn't want to appear foolish. Manchester raised his hand and pressed the play button.

On the screen, Sam gazed into the camera lens. "I think I can guarantee a confession before I'm done, but we'll come back to the topic of murder later."

Richard relaxed his stance, curious about how Sam intended to get that confession.

"So, you're wondering about the will, about who gets what. Yes, of course you are. Okay then, let's get started," he chuckled, taking his time.

Loren tapped her fingers against the arm of the couch in an impatient, muted thumping.

"Richard first. Richard, you've been by my side for two decades, protecting me and being a wonderful friend. You've lived in this house as long as I have. Stay. It's yours now, along with everything in it and enough money to cover the taxes, if you decide to keep it."

The house? Richard couldn't speak. Sandra shot him a glare of pure venom. She would be the one leaving, not him. But he felt like a fraud taking the house when he couldn't stop Sam from being murdered.

"Next come the kids. My sons Andrew and Sean; Sandy's kids Oliver and Megan; Loren and Oskar's kids Tim, Tegan and Tiffany … why you would name your kids in such a way I never understood … Daniel's daughter Maria; and Brent's kids Laura and Mark." A short pause and a mischievous smile. "To them, I leave all of my money, every penny divided equally and put in trust until they reach the age of twenty-one." Another pause. "That's right people, you aren't getting a cent."

Thoughts of murder were forgotten as the room exploded with outrage. Richard was quiet. Watching. Studying.

"I'll contest the will," Sandra spat, "see if I don't."

"That's right," Loren said. "He obviously wasn't in his right mind. Not his fault of course, that horrible disease."

Manchester raised his hands, trying to stop the conversation from running away. "I assure you, the will is legal. Sam made it while his mind was perfectly sound. You may contest it of course, but it will hold up in court. As Sam's executor and lawyer I'll make sure of that."

So the man did have some country lawyer in him. All the family members were on their feet, the noise increasing as each person tried to talk over the others. On screen Sam waited, not yet paused.

Unbelievable. Richard stepped forward and gave a long, shrill whistle. They turned toward him as one, staring at the outsider. "I think you've all forgotten Sam's accusation," he said. "One of you is a murderer."

Silence.

"He's right," Daniel admitted after a moment. "But whichever one of you killed my brother, your kids would still get their inheritance. Maybe that's why Sam did it this way."

"Whichever one of us?" Brent said. "What about you?"

"I loved my brother."

"And he was my best friend." Brent boomed.

The group degenerated into a storm of shouts and insults.

"Quiet," Sam yelled, waving his hand from side to side. "I'm not done."

Richard watched hope creep back onto their faces. Manchester had the remote pointed at the player but the group quieted enough to catch Sam's next words.

Sam mimicked, hands to his face. "Oh, why did he do this to us, his loving, loyal family?" He peered into the camera again. "You all thought I was a prize chump."

A mask of "who-me?" innocence was plastered on each face as they uncertainly retook their seats.

"Oh, I was a prize chump for a long time, honestly taking you all at face value. Then I discovered something." Another dramatic pause. "Brent, how long have you been banging my wife?"

Sandra and Brent glanced at each other, then away.

"Rhetorical question. At the time of this recording it's been two years, seven months and a few days."

Sandra muttered something again about contesting the will, but with less fire. Brent kept his eyes on the TV.

"Once I found out my wife and best friend weren't who I thought, I started examining the rest of you. My brother Daniel, always so grateful for the job at Carter's Chili and the chance to prove himself. Daniel, how much money have you stolen from me? By my calculations it's somewhere around two million dollars."

"I ... I didn't ... I ..." Daniel crept to the back of the room, away from all the eyes.

"That leaves Loren and Oskar. Oskar, it's obvious you hate chili, and Loren it's obvious you hate me," Sam chuckled at that bit of cleverness, "but, neither of those is as deplorable as, say, a long affair or embezzlement."

The couple sat straighter, an air of superiority in Loren as she scowled at the others.

"However, the two of you spent most of last year plotting the best way to kill me. You really should delete your e-mail messages more often. Loren, you're smarter than that."

Loren was on her feet, purple with rage.

"This disease must have seemed like a gift," Sam continued.

"That's right, you bastard," she spat, "and I hope it hurt like all hell was tearing you apart." Oskar's hand touched her arm and she dropped to the couch, glaring hatefully at Sam's image.

"Each one of you hurt me deeply, betrayed me. I hope you all have the self-respect to not deny the things I've said. Doesn't matter, the proof is in a sealed envelope in Manchester's possession."

The lawyer gave a brief nod of confirmation when they looked his way. On screen Sam held up his hands for peace. "Give me a few more minutes. We're not done yet and you will want to hear the rest." He took another drink.

The mood in the room was foul, everyone sitting in their own private gloom while staring at the television. With the secrets Sam had revealed any one of them would have been justified in storming out—or at least trying to get past Richard to leave. One of them had to see if they were revealed as the murderer. Did the others stay in hopes of getting a share of the as-yet-unmentioned company?

Sam took a deep breath and cleared his throat. "I guess you've seen the symptoms of CJD first hand. I sure hope so. The lack of coordination, muscle twitching, speech impairment. The confusion, disorientation, nervousness. Perhaps even personality changes and dementia."

Loren smiled at the list of symptoms.

"Variant CJD, the type I have, comes from eating contaminated meat products and is extremely rare. Less than a hundred people in the world have it. Do any of you wonder how I contracted such a rare disease?"

Pow! And that was it, Richard saw the whole picture. That's the murder Sam was talking about. Someone had infected Sam.

"Contaminated meat," Sam repeated. "It took me close to a year to track down the infected tissue samples I wanted. In the end, it was easier to get it from a man with the disease than from a cow." A pause. "I paid generously for that brain sample and brought it back home."

More finger thumping by Loren.

Where was Sam going with this? How would this expose the guilty person?

"Then I infected myself."

Loren's fingers stopped mid-drum. Everyone stared and Sam stared back. Out of the corner of his eye Richard could see Sandra turn to look at him. He knew she would have that smug smile on her face and thoughts of contesting the will in her head. It didn't matter. Richard felt sucker punched.

"Why would you do that?" Sam whispered in mock horror. "Fair question." He seemed to gather his thoughts, took a deep breath and continued. "I have a brain tumor. It's big, it's inoperable and it's killing me slowly."

Richard scrambled to catch up, the understanding he was so sure he had a moment ago had dissipated like smoke. He leaned against the wall beside the door.

"Before our next dinner, I'll be having an operation. My doctor will remove a chunk of my tumor … the part he can get to without killing me. I've told him it's for study by a private lab after I'm gone, and he assures me that I will still be able to function once it's removed."

"After that I will come home and work on a special batch of chili for our upcoming weekend. My last chili. And on that night each of you, except Richard of course, will eat the new recipe with my … special ingredient."

Special ingredient? What did—?

Loren lurched to her feet gagging, then vomited on the carpet in front of her. Tears flowed down her face as she made retching sounds again and again. "Bastard," she managed between heaves. "Bastard!"

"Yes, by the time you see this you will all have had exposure to a contaminated product … my own brain. It will be far too late to get it out of your system."

Manchester looked appalled and disgusted, the remote forgotten in his hand.

"Why would you do that?" Sam repeated in his whispered voice. "Well, I could have infected all of you with the sample instead of myself, but I want you to see the symptoms of this horrible disease as I die. I want you each to know what to look for in yourself. Mostly I want you all to hope that maybe, somehow, you are the one the disease will skip over."

Sandra got to her feet, sat down, then stood again, her hands pressed against the sides of her face.

"How about it?" Sam continued. "Any coordination problems? Slurred speech? Muscle twitching?"

"No!" Daniel shouted from the other side of the room. "No. Not me." He bolted for the door but before passing through it he stopped and turned back, a pleading, anxious look on his face. Was he hoping for a revelation that this was all a joke? A hoax punishment for their indiscretions?

The first stage of grief is denial.

"Now, one last item to take care of. I leave Carter's Chili, divided equally among you five betrayers. I imagine once word gets out that the executive board is dying of CJD the stock won't be worth a damn anyway."

Loren shot a glare of absolute loathing at her dead brother and turned for the door, sweeping a lamp off an end table as she went. At the exit she turned back, mouth open but no words coming, the fury obvious on her face.

Oskar headed for the bar in the corner, then stood there with a different, unopened bottle in each hand. His gaze of disbelief was fixed on the television.

"You couldn't have just divorced me?" Sandra wailed. "You …" She stopped, hearing the slur to her speech. Was it just the anger? She smoothed her blouse, turned and left the room.

Brent watched her go, quiet, making no effort to move or speak. One hand, clenched into a fist in front of his mouth, he waited for Sam to continue.

"So in the end, I wasn't only the killer, but the weapon as well." Sam said.

Richard got to his feet, heading for the door. He didn't need to hear any more, these words weren't for him. Still, as he passed Sandra, leaning against the wall outside the room, he could hear Sam's final words chasing him down the hallway.

"There's your murder, five of them actually, and the confession I promised too. Call the police, I won't run."

DARKHOUSE BOOKS

About Darkhouse Books:

Darkhouse Books is dedicated to publishing entertaining fiction, primarily in the mystery and science fiction field.

Darkhouse Books is located in Niles, California, an inadvertently-preserved, 120 year old rail town, forty miles from San Francisco. Further information may be obtained by visiting our website at www.darkhousebooks.com.

About this book:

The typeface in this book is 11.5 Garamond and Helvetica (for the headings). It was laid out using Adobe InDesign software and converted to PDF for uploading to the printing facility.

www.ingramcontent.com/pod-product-compliance
Lightning Source LLC
Chambersburg PA
CBHW021015120726
47905CB00009B/3027